Inner Passage
Collected Short Stories
Marlene Lee

Published by:
Experiments in Fiction
www.experimentsinfiction.com

ISBN: 9781739404468

Marlene Lee

INNER PASSAGE

Collected Short Stories

Marlene Lee

INNER PASSAGE

Collected Short Stories

Inner Passage

Collected Short Stories

Marlene Lee

Contents

INNER PASSAGE 8

VIRGIE 28

MYRTLE JENSEN 41

HEARTLAND 53

IF YOU LOVE A THING 79

PEN-AND-INK 98

THE CREEK 109

THE LONG BLACK CADILLAC 120

THE BROOM 124

CITY OF TOMORROW 130

THE JURY IS OUT 155

Publication Credits 197

Acknowledgements 198

For my dear friends
Jackie and Peter Michel
and every member of their family.

Inner Passage

The crash of lightning and thunder felt personal. She wouldn't have been surprised to smell sulfur or see a crack open up in the windshield.

Here under a giant oak it was dark. She couldn't read the road map spread out next to her. In the thick storm light, she'd taken a wrong exit off the highway as it ran through the woods and mountains. Now she was parked at the end of a dead-end road, only feet, she was sure, from the edge of a cliff. If the ground shook, she would go right over the edge, down, down into the valley below. Another wrong exit. The local police would shake their heads over the tall, fifty-ish woman who died in a North Carolina rainstorm in a car with California plates and a paint job scratched by a moaning tree.

In half-blind maneuvers, forward and reverse, she gained the opposite direction. As the '05 Lincoln rolled back along the wet road, the headlights brought a sign up and out of obscurity: The Inn and Conference Grounds of the South.

Rebecca parked in a lot across the road from a shuttered, two-story stone building partly hidden by woods, and stepped out of the car. The warm, humid wind pushed her toward the hotel porch lit by a single bulb swaying on a chain.

"Honey, all our rooms are booked," said the tired-looking woman in shadows behind the reservation desk. Rebecca tried to fluff her hair away from her temples where the rainwater had stuck it.

"I need a place to stay," she said, and was overcome by a fit of coughing.

"We have a conference this weekend that still has openings," the receptionist said without interest. She watched the tall woman dig in a little crocheted purse that was at odds with the Birkenstocks on her large feet. "You can register and stay in one of the dormitories." She pointed listlessly to the registration table.

But Rebecca veered off toward the bathroom. Behind the double swinging doors, over a sink stained brown from iron deposits, she placed a cough drop in her mouth, closed her eyes, and began to practice the deep breathing exercise her doctor had recommended. *Breathe. Hold. One, two, three.* Slowly fighting her way up through the syrup of anxiety, she lifted her head. The cough drop clicked against her back teeth. "I'll enroll in anything," she whispered to her reflection, "if they'll give me a room."

It was a writers' conference. She'd never heard of such a thing, but she signed a check drawn on her inheritance funds and was directed to a room on the second story of a stone dormitory. Crossing its dark interior courtyard, she suddenly stopped, frightened again by her own action, traveling across the country, searching for a life now that Mother was gone. She should have stayed at home on the orchard north of Sacramento, safe and comfortable, sleeping late, shopping, going to the movies, as she had done for fifty years.

What could have possessed her to drive three thousand miles, only to find herself blundering into a building that meant nothing to her?

What could have possessed her to fritter away fifty years?

She stepped up through the stairwell to the balcony overlooking the courtyard and carried her suitcase to a plain room with an open closet and no dressing table; a room without comfort, very unlike home. The damp breeze blowing in through the window screen could not dry the rainwater on the sill. The single bulb could not light the room. She opened the door to the bathroom and snapped on another low-watt bulb. At least there was a cabinet above the sink. As she was arranging her medicines, a second door to the bathroom opened and a young man burst in.

"Pardon me!" He backed out of the bathroom into an adjoining room that looked as dim as her own. She locked his door from the inside and began lining up her special soap, disinfectants, ointments, creams, pills, sprays, and inhaler. There was another flurry of activity at the young man's door, then a polite knock.

"Yes?" Rebecca opened the door.

This time it was a young woman, very young, perhaps eighteen or nineteen. Rebecca envied her silky blonde hair, undyed, and the moist skin of a person who still manufactures her own estrogen. The woman introduced herself as Darla. "We have a shared bathroom," she said in a Southern accent, and, after studying Rebecca with a mixture of doubt and pity, began to explain the locks.

"See this?" She stepped aside so that Rebecca could watch her depress the little button in the center of the doorknob. "You press it in, then press again to release it." She crossed to Rebecca's door. "Yours works the same way." She illustrated and returned to her door. "Let's practice. I'll go back in my room, then you lock the door."

Rebecca followed instructions.

"See?" Darla called out from the other side of the door. "You've locked it." She wiggled the doorknob. "I can't get in."

Rebecca was less interested in the lock than in the young woman. "Are you here for the writers' conference, Darla?"

There was a muffled sound, then, more clearly, "Unlock the door."

Rebecca opened the door.

"I'm not here for the conference, but my husband is." Darla wore shorts and a halter-type blouse with embroidery and pretty buttons. "Do you mind if I splash water on my face? It will just take a second."

Through the frosted bathroom window open at the top, Rebecca could hear fresh gusts of rain blowing along the balcony. She resumed the arrangement of her medicines and creams and listened to the brisk splashing.

Darla dried her face. "My goodness you have a lot of medications."

"I have several doctors," Rebecca said with modesty.

Darla hung up the towel. She looked as if she wanted to touch the collection, but instead she said, "Are you here for the writers' conference, too?"

"Yes, I guess I am," said Rebecca.

"My husband, Timmy, is a writer. He's written hundreds of pages."

Rebecca popped a calcium tablet in her mouth. "Are you from North Carolina?"

"Yes," said Darla. "Both of us are."

Rebecca chewed thoughtfully. "What do people do in writers' conferences, Darla?"

"Write, I guess. I'm only here because Timmy's here. Are you literary?"

Rebecca didn't know what the girl was talking about. She swallowed the calcium. "I don't think so."

"Did you pick up your folder at the registration table? It tells you how to become an author. Well, I'll be seeing you. Timmy and I will make sure we don't lock you out of the bathroom." Darla depressed and released the lock once more for Rebecca's benefit, and closed the door behind her.

Early the next morning Rebecca, wearing walking shorts and a ruffled blouse Mother had bought her, took a seat at a long table in the back of her assigned classroom. She'd read the schedule and she liked to be early. The rustic stone building was quiet, the hallways still. She stared through the rippling glass of the old windows at the perfect blue sky washed clean by last night's rain and filled here and there with—she tried to think like a writer. "Clouds" was too ordinary. "Clouds of marshmallow." Yes. Marshmallows and whipped cream. The words reminded her of home; of the rich, soft, airy life she'd led before Mother died. Marshmallows in hot chocolate. Cream over peaches fresh from the orchard. Homesickness swept through her and made her weak. She gripped the edge of the table. Then, as so often happened, the thing she was holding onto buckled. The table collapsed. She, herself, was disintegrating.

She struggled against the anxiety attack. Her therapist had told her to fill nothingness with sensory exercises. Fill herself with something that brings comfort and takes up space. She glanced desperately about the empty classroom, as empty as she herself, for a commodity; a filler. She remembered the whipped cream and, in her imagination, began spooning it into her vacancy. She toiled for several minutes. But though she began to feel better, she hated the exercise. Breathing hard, she looked out the window. Through the uneven old glass, a distant clock tower rose above the tops of trees. Everywhere, green leaves were fresh and bright.

She glanced away. There was something specific she should be worrying about, but she didn't know what it was.

The bathroom door. She'd forgotten to unlock Darla and Timmy's side of the bathroom. Hugging her lined paper tablet and conference folder to her chest, she jumped up and hurried out of the building. Once she reached the green woods she began to run. She imagined Darla and Timmy pounding to be let in, desperate with a bodily emergency, despising her for carelessness. At the dormitory she planted her large feet on every other step of the stairwell, sprinted along the balcony, her walking shorts flapping about her white thighs, inserted the key into the lock, and burst into her room. She reached the bathroom, drenched in sweat, and released the button in the center of the doorknob. She heard quarreling on the other side of the door.

"It's just a story!" Darla was shouting. Silence. Taut, vibrating silence. Rebecca stood behind the bathroom door and waited for someone to say something.

"He's not necessarily writing about *you!*" Darla snapped. It sounded like a telephone conversation. "Timmy is a wonderful person and he's *my husband.* You shouldn't have been going through his notebooks! With all the authors in the world, why did you have to pick *him* to read?"

How terrible to be a writer, Rebecca thought. Once you write something, people read it. She slowly backed out of the bathroom and, exhausted from the run, sat down at her plain desk nailed into the dormitory wall. She ran a finger along the pink rubber binding at the top of her writing tablet. So many blank pages. She supposed she was going to have to write something on them. Unless, of course, she left the conference now. The whole day stretched ahead of her. Hours and hours of daylight driving. Even while she thought about packing up the contents of the medicine chest and leaving the Inn and Conference Grounds of the South, she took out the pen that had been provided and experimented with a sentence: *"Mother died three months ago. I loved her more than anybody."*

She was astounded by the words and ran for her inhaler. When she returned, the words were still there. She covered them with the folder. They were too personal. She could not bear to see them.

She lay down on the narrow bed and practiced breathing. She was not going to be able to write a word. Not a word about Mother. It brought on anxiety. Not any other words, either. She couldn't write a mystery story because she didn't know anything about crime. Couldn't write about love or sex because she didn't know anything about

men. She didn't understand politics. And she couldn't write a memoir because she didn't have a life.

A headache struck her between the eyes, but when she tried to open the bathroom door to get an aspirin, it was locked. She knocked. There was no answer. She went onto the balcony, blinking in the bright sunlight, and knocked on Darla and Timmy's door. Darla, looking as if she'd been to a funeral, answered.

"I'm sorry to bother you," Rebecca said, "but my bathroom door's locked."

"Oh, dear," said Darla. Holding a handkerchief to her streaming eyes, she entered the bathroom and opened Rebecca's door.

Rebecca touched Darla's shoulder awkwardly. "You look very unhappy."

Darla sobbed into her handkerchief.

"How long have you been married, Darla?"

"Two weeks."

"Two weeks isn't very long." Rebecca didn't know what else to say. That was the extent of her knowledge about marriage.

"My husband wrote certain things about my mother, and Mother read them."

"What kinds of things?"

"Mean things." Darla blew her nose and promptly embarked on a fresh fit of crying. "But Mother shouldn't read his stories! They're his private property until the world publishes them!"

Rebecca entered the bathroom. "You're lucky your mother's alive," she said. "My mother died three months ago." She walked to the medicine cabinet and shook an aspirin into the palm of her hand.

"I'm sorry to hear that." Darla's eyes were on the bottle of aspirin. "How do you keep all those pills and things cool when the car gets hot?" she asked.

"I carry my medicines in a picnic cooler," Rebecca said, proud of her thorough planning. It had been her own idea. She closed the cabinet door and, looking in the mirror, asked Darla, "What mean things does he write?"

"That Mother's bossy."

Rebecca filled a glass with water, threw back her head, and swallowed the pill. "Is she?"

"Yes. But he makes it sound worse than it is."

"Writing is hard," said Rebecca. "It's hard to make things sound right, at least the way you mean them to. I tried it a minute ago. That's why I came for an aspirin." The conversation ended and they each went into their room, being careful to leave the bathroom doors unlocked.

Rebecca sat down at her desk and added a tentative sentence: "Mother loved me more than anybody, too." She read and reread her words, but she didn't know how to turn them into a story.

That's what the writer's conference was about: stories. The brochure said so.

By now the daily writing class would be nearly over, so there was no point in going back. She lay down on her single bed and stared at the ceiling, wondering what it would feel like to write something about Mother that wasn't nice; for instance, that she was bossy. A few minutes after she'd heard Darla's footsteps going along the balcony and down the stairwell, there was a knock on the door. It was Timmy.

"Excuse me, ma'am," he said politely, his southern speech low and musical. "I've locked myself out of the room." With the sunlight shining on his glossy brown hair he seemed more like an engaging boy than a married man. Rebecca opened her bathroom door so he could go through the passage. As he walked by the desk he saw her handwriting. "What are you working on?"

Rebecca covered her words with the folder. "Nothing."

"I'm writing about my—well, someone I know," Timmy offered. "They say 'write what you know.'" He opened his folder. "Do you want to hear it?"

Rebecca nodded. Her chair scraped against the plank floor as she moved to face him.

"*The Queen of Night*," he began, "*descended into the open mouth of hell that spewed flames and hot coals, dragging her daughter and muscular yet innocent son-in-law behind her.*"

"My," said Rebecca, leaning forward. "You paint quite a picture."

"*Her cackle raised the hackles of anyone listening,*" he continued, and proceeded to read the part where the Queen of Night dies a tortuous death as the beautiful daughter escapes with the aid of her muscular yet innocent husband.

"True story," Timmy said. Rebecca caught her breath.

"Just kidding." He stared thoughtfully down at his thongs and flexed his feet. A little patch of dark hair grew on the top of each toe. He didn't look particularly muscular to Rebecca.

He was young and slim, like Darla. Short, too. Rebecca was taller than both of them. Older, too, of course.

"You don't mind if I confide in you, do you?" he asked.

Rebecca was flattered. She didn't tell him she wasn't a writer. Timmy shook back his wavy, jaw-length hair. "It's based on my mother-in-law. Darla doesn't see her objectively. When Darla reads the entire story"—he held up his manuscript—"she'll see her mother for what she really is."

"So when the mother dies, that's not the end of the story?"

"That's only the beginning," Timmy said prophetically.

"Why don't you like her?"

"She calls Darla every night and tells her to leave me."

"How long has Darla's mother known you?"

"Three months." Timmy's left eye moved slightly out of focus. "When I have a best-seller she'll change her tune."

Rebecca was beset by a memory of Mother's amiable laugh when, at age eighteen, she'd said, "I want to go to college and have a job someday. I want to find a husband."

"You were never good in school, Becky," Mother had replied. "If you stay at home on the orchard, the right man will find you."

But he never did.

"Tell Darla not to listen to her mother," she said to Timmy. "Tell her to just go ahead and live." The effort cost her. She began to breathe rapidly.

Timmy's wandering eye snapped back into focus. "I've told her!" he almost yelped. "It doesn't do any good!" He thumped the manuscript, jumped up from the edge of the bed, and began backing toward the bathroom door. "Darla cries all the time. If her mother doesn't stop criticizing me, our marriage will be shorter than the writers' conference."

Rebecca put her hand to her racing heart. "Maybe you could write a story about you and Darla instead of your mother-in-law," she whispered.

"No, I don't think so." His left eye strayed again. "Until her mother improves, there is no Darla and me," and he strode through the bathroom to his room, shutting both doors loudly behind him.

Rebecca turned her chair around and faced her desk. The sharp point of the lead pencil landed almost of its own accord.

"The woman who lived on the orchard loved her daughter, and her daughter loved her," Rebecca wrote. "Never did a cross word pass between them."

She experienced her usual bad nerves and anxiety as she walked to class, in and out of the morning sunlight that lay puddled on the forest floor. When she remembered that she might be called on to say something, or worse, show what she'd written, she turned and ran back through the trees for her inhaler, which gave her a chance to double-check the bathroom door. She returned to the path that led through the green woods. A mourning dove, followed by a three-whistle, one-note bird she couldn't name, sang out. The air was humid and still.

The class discussed Timmy's manuscript first. "Mythic figures," said Professor Wyandotte in the silence that followed the final writhing screams of the *Queen of Night*.

"Possibly science fiction genre. Is this your first draft?" Professor Wyandotte was old and frail, with shoulder blades that looked like roots of wings worn down to the nubbin. He made gestures in the air that didn't seem to match what he was talking about. Rebecca understood very little of what he said. He asked Timmy to re-read the opening lines.

"The Queen of Night descended into the open mouth of hell that spewed—"

The story did not sound as good to Rebecca the second time around. The class didn't like it. Following an acrimonious discussion, one of the other students read a story, and nobody liked it, either. Arguing took up the rest of the class time and Rebecca didn't have to read.

Walking back to the dormitory she once again considered leaving the conference. Not only was her story a single paragraph, in contrast to other students' endless pages, but it was written in pencil on lined paper. Everyone else had typed theirs. Everyone else had a computer. She decided to stay one more day. But first thing tomorrow morning, as soon as she heard the little three-whistle, one-note bird, she would drive away in a southerly direction—assuming she could find south—and leave writing behind. She had a cousin in Florida.

She spent the rest of the day reading a romance novel in bed. Around eight o'clock, in the orange light of sunset that filled her room, Rebecca heard a knock on the bathroom door.

"Rebecca?" It was Darla standing in the doorway, the last of the sun burnishing her blonde hair. "I have a terrible blister on my foot. Do you have something in your medicine cabinet for blisters?"

Rebecca got out of bed, walked into the bathroom, and directed the young woman to sit on the edge of the tub while she washed, then treated the blister with one of her preparations.

"Timmy's upset about the criticism of his story," Darla said, twisting her ankle so Rebecca could get to the heel.

"The class didn't like it very much," Rebecca murmured.

"He's too brilliant for them," Darla said.

Rebecca straightened and returned the ointment to the medicine cabinet.

"I wish we'd never come to this conference."

"Me, too," agreed Rebecca. "I'm only here because I needed a place to stay. I've had more anxiety attacks in North Carolina than in all the rest of my travels put together."

"You're not a writer?" Darla asked, surprised.

"Not at all," said Rebecca. "I'm on a trip across America."

"How far have you traveled?"

"From California."

"Why?"

Rebecca looked at herself in the mirror. She lowered her head several inches, then quickly straightened because the roots were showing gray again. "I wanted experience," she said, ashamed of telling the truth. "Until this trip, I've never had any."

"Everybody has experience," said Darla. "Just sitting in one place is an experience."

But Rebecca wasn't interested in fine points. "I've never had any experience of my own."

"Don't you have friends?"

"They all moved away after graduation."

"Couldn't you make new ones?"

Rebecca knelt on the floor to apply the Band–Aid. "It was easier to stay at home with Mother. Anyway, that's what she wanted me to do, and I always did what Mother wanted." She looked up into Darla's face and blushed. "I met a nice man recently. His name is Raymond."

"Where did you meet him?"

Rebecca got to her feet. "On a bench in Missoula, Montana."

"A bench?"

"A bench on the university campus. That's where he likes to sit and grade papers. He's a teacher."

Darla reached down to her heel and idly smoothed the Band–Aid.

"But Mother told me to forget about him."

"How can your mother tell you to forget about him? Your mother's dead."

"Sometimes I still hear her talk."

"Mothers never stop talking," agreed Darla. "And if they're like my mother, they're usually right." Her hands flew to her face and she cried out in a despairing voice, "I shouldn't have married Timmy!" She looked as if she might faint backwards into the tub.

Rebecca reached down to smooth Darla's hair. Her forehead was clammy. "You've only been married two weeks," she reminded the girl.

"Oh, Timmy! Timmy!" Darla sobbed.

Rebecca's heart began to race, but it wasn't anxiety about herself. She was afraid for Darla. The child mustn't return home. She tried to think what Mother would do if she were here.

"Let's go shopping," she said desperately.

Darla seemed stupefied by the suggestion.

"Want to go shopping?" Rebecca repeated.

"Why?"

"That's what my mother would do."

"Isn't that avoiding the problem?"

"Well, yes," Rebecca admitted. "Mother and I always avoided problems."

Darla dried her tears and stood up. "Excuse me for saying so, but your mother doesn't sound very mature."

Rebecca had never thought of Mother as mature or im-mature. She was simply Mother. "The main thing about my mother was that she knew best what people should do and so everyone did it. Is that immature?"

"That's bossy," said Darla.

Rebecca's heart raced faster. She expected another anxiety attack but felt angry loyalty instead. "My mother was a wonderful woman," she informed Darla stoutly. "You didn't know her so you can't say what kind of woman she was."

Darla bent her knee and screwed her head around to look at the bandaged heel. "At least my mother's mature."

"All right, Miss Know-It-All!" Rebecca suddenly shouted. "My mother might have been immature. And she was bossy! But so is yours! I can tell from listening that your mother is immature and bossy!" Rebecca felt her chest fill, not with anxiety, but with a thawing of something old and crusty. She looked into Darla's startled eyes, looked so deeply that she felt she was looking into herself. "Don't wait until your mother dies to—live," she breathed.

Darla's eyes narrowed. "I don't need your advice. You're not my mother." And she wheeled out of the room. Upstairs, someone turned on a faucet. The pipes screeched. The lovely flood in Rebecca's chest dried up. Darla was right. She was the last person on earth to give advice. Hating herself for her fifty years of obedience, she turned and scanned the medicine cabinet for a pill that would make her feel better.

Just after midnight, Rebecca padded to the bathroom. Half-asleep, she used the toilet, rinsed her hands, and left by—the wrong door. She stopped, frozen in the doorway. Darla and Timmy were so busy making love, the single bulb still on, that they didn't hear her. They'd forgotten to lock their door from the room side, and so Rebecca saw them face each other, kneel on the bed, kiss and work together until, by some kind of mysterious agreement, they lay back on their pillows, arms around each other, tense and still, until, by more agreement, they began to move once again. They seemed much older than eighteen and nineteen.

Rebecca was transfixed. She should have immediately closed the door, but didn't. Their nakedness shocked and aroused her. Moaning, half-singing together, Darla and Timmy were very different at night than they were in the daytime. Mother had been wrong about sex. Some people enjoy it.

She closed the door carefully and returned to her room. Flushed and overheated, she sat down at the desk and pulled the writing tablet toward her. Through mounting cries in the next room, she wrote a sentence. She stopped and listened, but the sounds trailed off like something moving away from her into the distance. Outside the old stone dormitory, crickets took up the slack and made another kind of sound on their dry, brittle instruments. A languid breeze blew across the windowsill. Rebecca applied herself to the writing tablet and produced another sentence. When she finished, she carefully removed the sheet from its pink rubber binding and returned to bed.

The next day after class she followed the sunlit balcony around to her room, entered, and found the bathroom locked. She stepped out onto the balcony again and knocked on Darla and Timmy's door. Timmy opened it.

"Have you seen Darla?" he asked. His left eye had moved off-center again.

"No, but can you unlock the door?"

"Sorry," he said, and stepped into the bathroom. But he stopped abruptly. "What the ...?"

Over his shoulder Rebecca saw the medicine cabinet door standing wide open. Every medicine bottle, every jar, every tube was gone. After one stunned moment Timmy turned, ran back into the room, and flung open empty drawers. He leaned on the bureau, arms braced like a man who is going to be sick.

"She left," he said.

Rebecca took a sideways step into the bathroom and examined the shelves, unwilling to believe Darla had stolen from her. In the bedroom Timmy began throwing clothes and books into a pack. "Can you give me a lift to the bus station?" he asked.

Rebecca felt an attack of something coming on, but since her medicines were gone, she didn't have to decide which one to take. By the time she'd finished packing—without her medicines it didn't take long—she felt better. Timmy was waiting for her in the parking lot. They drove silently to the station. He took his pack out of the back seat and came around to the driver's side. Through the window he shook Rebecca's large, spotted hand. Then, impulsively, his sky-blue eyes filling with tears, he lowered his head, laid it sideways in the open window, and gave Rebecca a kiss on the cheek. "I wish you were my mother-in-law," he said.

"Where are you going, Timmy?"

"To find Darla." He straightened up and pulled cash out of his pocket. Rebecca waved him away, but he thrust some bills into her hand. "It won't cover all your medicine."

"No, please," Rebecca said. "Darla's frightened. She was just trying to fortify herself."

Timmy's left eye wandered out of focus, then centered again. He replaced the money in his pocket and disappeared into the bus station, a muscular yet innocent young man. Rebecca sat in the car and cried. She so hoped Darla and Timmy would stay together. Opening her crocheted purse, she re-read the sentences she'd written last night while crickets sang in the darkness and Darla and Timmy made love: "Dear Raymond, Do you remember me, the woman from California? We met at your bench in Missoula. We ate dinner together and talked. I am coming back to Missoula. Do you want to see me? Sincerely, Rebecca Quint."

She replaced the letter in its envelope, sealed it, stamped it, and dropped it in the mailbox on the corner. Then she got back in her car and set off on what she hoped was the road to Montana.

Virgie

On an afternoon in spring, 1923, Virgie Johnston is about to be picked up from the country school by her parents and driven to town for a social call on the banker's wife, Mrs. Messick. Ninety years later, the banker's house will seem small and shabby where it occupies a corner lot in Oakley. The town, too, will be much diminished. But in 1923 the house is one of the nicest in Oakley. Its wrap-around porch, double parlor, and indoor plumbing make Virgie proud to live in the same county.

"Remember, Mrs. Messick may live in a fine home in town but she isn't afraid to get her hands dirty," Virgie's father says. "Don't let anyone tell you different. She does her own housework and gardening. Nobody does it for her." Virgie thinks about this while she collects eggs or helps him at the milk separator in the cyclone cellar. "No matter what people say," he adds, his slow speech a notch faster, "your mother works hard, too. She may call on the banker's and doctor's wives in town, she may write poetry and read books, but she works hard on the farm."

Only recently has Virgie begun to feel wary of her mother's reputation. People compliment the rest of the family—the father and four children—on being "common." Uncle Jim, who lives with them, is too eccentric to be labeled either common or proud. But Martha Johnston, they say, puts on airs.

Every week, usually on a Wednesday or Thursday, Martha asks her husband to drive her from their farm nine miles west and four miles south of Oakley into town where she will call on women friends. Pausing in the afternoon to make tea, the town women are distracted from their housekeeping by a farm woman who, some say, won't stay home on the farm. Martha Johnston is not only uppity, they say; she gives women an excuse to waste time as they put down their brooms, powder their faces, and carry cups and saucers into parlors not meant to be used on weekdays.

"Want to walk home together?" one of Virgie's friends whispers during history class. "I'm not supposed to be alone with the boys anymore."

"I can't," Virgie whispers back. "I'm riding into Oakley with my parents today."

The girl twists in her desk and looks Virgie in the eye. "Calling on the banker's wife? Your mother's not a town woman. No amount of putting on airs will change that." The girl faces forward again because the teacher is watching and because she doesn't have adequate words to convey the layer of contempt lying beneath their friendship. Virgie has seen the scorn in the girl's eye. *No amount of putting on airs will change that* are not eighth-grade words. They are borrowed from grown-ups and they hold a trough full of criticism.

That same afternoon Dave Johnston stops the car in front of the Messick house and says to his wife as she steps over the running board and down onto the gravel, "I'll be finished at the feed store in an hour. Watch for me."

Martha restrains a wave of chestnut-red hair coming free of a hairpin. "We might not be finished," she says before turning and proceeding up the walk. "Mrs. Messick is enrolled in a study course from the college. There's a lot to talk about."

"Well," Dave says, not a man to lay down an ultimatum, "watch for me, anyway. I'll be back in an hour."

Inside, the Messick house is cool and restful. Colored bits of light from a stained-glass window in the west wall play across the velvet-covered sofa.

"Did you remember the book?" Mrs. Messick asks Martha, handing her a cup of tea.

Martha takes a dog-eared copy of *Favorite Poems by Great Authors of the World* from her purse.

"I wish I had your literary interests," says Mrs. Messick. "I can't even keep a diary." She glances at Virgie. "Your mother has beautiful handwriting, you know."

Virgie wonders what it would be like to have a mother who doesn't have beautiful handwriting, doesn't keep a diary, doesn't write poetry. Her mother, a quiet woman at home, becomes public and talented when she reads her verses at Christmas, Easter, and graduation exercises.

When Virgie is halfway through her cocoa she hears her mother say, "Do you know of a place in town where my daughter and I can stay in September?"

Mrs. Messick can't hide her surprise. Virgie drains her cocoa and puts down the cup.

"What do you mean, a place for us to stay?" she whispers as Mrs. Messick passes through the arched doorway into the dining room and on into the kitchen.

Her mother straightens Virgie's collar, plucks at the shirtwaist swelling slightly over budding breasts. "Your father and I want you to take a year of school in town. It will be a chance we never had."

Virgie lifts her cup from the doily and studies the chocolate sediment at the bottom. She takes a sudden dislike to the flowered china. *I don't want to go to school in Oakley,* she wants to say. *I don't want to write poetry or take study courses or have beautiful handwriting.*

Virgie can tell her father important things about herself that she cannot tell her mother. His blue eyes absorb as much light as she cares to let shine, but her mother's ideal face, perfectly smooth and oval, squares up now and her eyes seem to pull close together.

"You don't know what you might want," she says just before Mrs. Messick reappears and sits down again on the sofa.

Virgie asks if she can take a walk. Her mother says that will be fine but to be back before her father returns from the feed store.

Oakley's gravel streets send up a fine white dust that powders Virgie's shoes and socks by the time she reaches the corner. The nearly ankle-length hem of her skirt is white with it. She turns the corner and continues on past small houses and vacant lots high with grass and weeds.

Children are playing in a front yard, going in and out of a pup tent from the war. The Messicks' son was killed in the Great War. Mrs. Messick often cries quietly in church during the Lord's Prayer.

The Oakley High School is up ahead. As Virgie draws closer, it doesn't seem to be an Oakley building anymore. It turns a face toward her and says it knows her, but she doesn't think so. Still, she suspects it's going to have something to do with her. She doesn't have much choice. It does know her.

She turns another corner and walks toward the feed store. Her parents' Ford is parked in the street. She opens the door and picks up the dust rag her mother keeps on the floor of the back seat for wiping barnyard dirt and Oakley's gravel powder from the family's shoes.

Her father is talking to Mr. Fink, the owner of the feed store. Virgie breathes in the field-and-barn-scented motes floating through the air, and coughs.

"Is your mother still busy?" her father asks. Virgie nods. She sits down on a plump feed bag and begins drawing circles in the dust from grain and hay that is always sifting onto the pine floor.

"Your daughter's growing up to be pretty smart," Mr. Fink says. Virgie looks at her father who has already turned his sky-blue eyes in her direction. His gaze is serious. She returns to the swirled lines beside her foot and busies herself drawing and disturbing the dust. When her father says, "Let's go, Puddin'," she runs her shoe through the marks and follows him outside.

At the car he stops. Resting one foot on the running board, he pulls a pocket watch from the bib of his overalls and says, "It hasn't been an hour yet." He crosses his arms and squints at the sun already beginning to slide down the western quarter.

"Am I going to school in Oakley in September?" Virgie asks.

Mr. Fink comes to the door and watches a mass of clouds gathering to the north. Her father is watching them, too.

"We'd better get home before that storm cloud does," he says. Inside the car he starts the engine and adjusts the choke. As the choppy motor conveys them along Second Street, Dave Johnston says, "You're a good student."

"I know," says Virgie.

"The country boys are pretty rough," he adds when he has stopped and put on the brake in front of the Messick house.

"I don't want to go to school in Oakley."

"It's up to your mother."

Virgie flares. "Why?"

Her father subdues her with a penetrating look into the back seat. "You have to keep pearls away from swine," he tells her. "That's in the Bible. Go get your mother and tell her we need to stay ahead of the weather."

With rain spattering the north window, the Johnstons sit down to pot roast, cooked carrots and potatoes, gravy, bread and butter, and canned plums in a Mason jar brought up from the cellar. It is still too early for the garden to produce.

"Is Virgie going to start school in Oakley next year?" Velma, the little sister, asks. Her chestnut-red hair bounces this way and that as she glances around the table.

"We have to find a place to stay first," says Martha.

"You're going to live in Oakley?" asks Adrian, the first-born.

"No," says Virgie, but she looks uncertainly at her mother.

"It remains to be seen," her father says. A clap of thunder makes the gravy quiver. The room needs light but they will finish supper before bringing out the kerosene lamp.

Uncle Jim folds his hands. Audie, the younger boy, looks thoughtfully at Virgie. They all know she's the best student in the family.

"The boys out here are rough," Martha says.

"No more rough than Oakley boys," says Adrian, eating methodically.

"Oakley boys are courteous," insists his mother.

Adrian looks doubtful and continues to chew.

"Am I going to live in Oakley, too?" Velma asks brightly, wriggling in her seat.

But her parents don't answer. As the light lessens and the checkered oil cloth loses its red-and-white, Velma stokes the conversation for color and interest.

"Uncle Jim, tell us about the time Miss Holshire proposed."

Uncle Jim crosses his knife and fork and folds his hands across his stomach. "'Mr. Johnston,' Miss Holshire says, 'let's get married.'

"'Don't be silly, Miss Holshire,' says I. 'Who would have us?'"

Velma laughs. Uncle Jim uncrosses his silverware and resumes eating.

"Miss Holshire says we put on airs," Audie says.

"Miss Holshire doesn't know her head from a bucket," says Uncle Jim.

"Miss Holshire is jealous," says Martha. Virgie hears her mother sniff once. It's not because she needs a hankie. If she did, she would turn her head away from the table and blow neatly into embroidered linen. "And she's backward, besides."

"As her proposal makes clear." Uncle Jim folds his hands again. Adrian chews. Virgie plays with her food.

Audie speaks up sharply. "What's 'airs'?"

"Pretensions," says Uncle Jim, and leaves the table. He comes and goes as he pleases. Their father says everyone should leave him alone. He more than makes up for his strangeness by the amount of work he can do.

It's the second time in the same day that Virgie has heard the phrase "putting on airs." It worries her that there might be another Martha Johnston she hasn't known about.

"People are just jealous," Martha repeats. "They're afraid of quality."

Everyone sees that Audie is about to ask what "qual–ity" means, and so they quickly find something else to talk about, leaving the boy to sit uncomfortably between dimpled Velma and preoccupied Virgie.

When the dishes are done Virgie leaves the kitchen, now bright with kerosene lamplight and smelling a little like the Ford, and goes upstairs to the southeast bed–room she and Velma share. She sits on the edge of their bed. Through the open window she hears the windmill squeaking. The last of the rain drips from the eaves. She wipes water off the windowsill with the tail of her skirt. Her face feels hot. She thinks she might have a fever. The wash house at the end of the path leading to the barnyard looks diminished in the darkness, as if it, too, has been talked about by people who say it really isn't a wash house, which it had thought all along it was.

On her way downstairs and out to get a dipperful of water from the well that is tucked down between the legs of the windmill, Virgie feels an almost uncontrollable love for the farm and everything on it now that she might have to live in Oakley. She senses that the present will not always be here; that it can be washed away, like the wooden plank over the creek. She would like to kiss the windmill, the wash house, the gate, the hen house, the barn. She would like to climb every tree and building. She wants to leap into the cattle trough.

She hears her mother returning from the outhouse along the path west of the garden. Her father goes out to meet her by the hollyhocks. In the silence between them, Virgie can almost hear the garden coming up.

"Mr. and Mrs. Messick offered to keep Virgie in town for the school year," she hears her mother say. "I could stay with her during the week and you could pick us up on Fridays."

In the dark, Virgie has trouble hanging the dipper back on the nail.

"You'd be gone for the week?" her father says.

"I can't leave her alone in town, Dave."

"Even with all those courteous Oakley boys?" He laughs quietly and makes a moist noise. Martha catches her breath. Virgie's parents fall silent before they begin whispering, light wind through the hollyhocks. Virgie waits until they go in the house before she follows them. She removes her shoes and climbs the stairs to the second floor. She can hear them downstairs moving about in their bedroom. She hates them. Her mother wants her to go to school in Oakley and her father is willing to send her away from the farm.

"How come the boys in Oakley aren't rough?" Audie asks next morning at breakfast.

Since their father doesn't answer, Adrian says, "Oakley boys are just as rough as we are." He borrows a phrase he's learned from adults. "I don't know where people get their facts."

"Am I rough?" asks Audie.

"Not yet," says Adrian, his forehead broad and bland, "but at the first sign, it's off to Oakley with you."

Audie puts his head between his hands, his thinking position. Martha taps him on the arm and he removes his elbows from the table.

Velma slams the screen door behind her and lands in her place at the table. "I just heard the church bell in Oakley ringing!"

"You can't hear it this far away," says Adrian.

"I did, too! It rang eight times when I was coming back from the outhouse!"

"Hush," says Martha. "We don't talk about the outhouse at the table."

Dave takes his pocket watch from the bib of his overalls. "It couldn't have rung eight times. It's only seven o'clock."

"Well, then the Oakley clock's broken," says Velma.

Dave snaps the watch shut and studies Virgie as he returns it to his overalls pocket. "Have some fried potatoes," he says.

"I'm not hungry." Virgie studies her empty plate. "I have a fever."

Martha lays the cool back of her hand against Virgie's cheek. "You don't feel feverish." Her father extends his hand, too, but Virgie draws away from both of them and leaves the table.

Outside, Uncle Jim is helping himself to a dipperful of well water. "Morning, Virgie."

"Good morning, Uncle Jim."

Uncle Jim hangs the dipper back on the nail. He opens the gate and starts across the barnyard toward the tractor parked by the shed.

"Virgie?" Her father comes walking toward the windmill from the house. When he's standing next to her, he cups his hand under her chin. "I guess you're thinking about Oakley."

Over his shoulder Virgie sees her mother step through the kitchen door. Martha unties her apron and drapes it over the mop handle leaning against the house. Beside her, the handle gains dignity, as if it were a coat tree instead of a mop. Bruno, the farm dog, feeds noisily at the dish near her feet.

"We could all live in Oakley during the week and come home on Saturday and Sunday," Virgie says without looking at her father.

"That wouldn't be practical," he says.

"Uncle Jim could take care of the farm," she insists. They both turn and watch Uncle Jim climb up onto the tractor.

"You'd leave him alone on the farm all week?" her father asks.

Virgie takes care not to look away from the tractor. "You'd leave me in town!" Hot tears spill onto her shirt-waist. "Let's all stay on the farm," she sobs. "We can stay here always. We don't need Oakley."

Dave's darkening eyes admit no light. "Your mother needs it," he says. Martha re-enters the house and Dave turns and follows the sound of the screen door closing.

Virgie watches him before she, too, turns and walks toward Uncle Jim who, by now, has gotten the John Deere started. He is seated high above the ground. Slowly he turns the tractor toward acreage lying along what will one day be called the old highway. The new highway, Interstate 70, will be constructed in the 1950s and completely bypass Oakley.

Adrian will become an engineer; Audie, a teacher. Velma will be killed in an automobile accident when she is sixteen. Virgie will graduate from Kansas Wesleyan University, marry a doctor from Salina, and die at thirty-nine of encephalitis. Dave Johnston will bleed to death in a farming accident, one leg cut off in the combine. Martha Johnston will outlive her husband and three of her four children. Her grief and copious handwritten diaries will accompany her to her ninety-seventh year. Uncle Jim will move off the farm when it is sold and spend the last twelve years of his life in a rented room in Oakley. One of Virgie's daughters will live in Seattle, San Francisco, and finally New York City where, driven by restless ambition and an effort to understand herself, she spends her days writing stories, some of which may trigger a hushed recognition: Ah, yes, that is the world and the people in it.

Myrtle Jensen

On these nice spring mornings my son likes to sit out on the front porch and watch the cars go by. Across the street there's a park. That's one of the reasons we bought this house, the park. There's a picnic table or two and some play equipment off to one side. Cars aren't allowed to park at the curb, so he has a good view of people sitting at the table eating take-out during their lunch hour. My son is particularly interested when boys come and throw their bikes down on the grass. Usually they're too old for the jungle gym and swings, but they're hanging onto boyhood habits even when their voices are changing.

Jeff's voice began to change the summer Mrs. Myrtle Jensen came to help us. He was getting a little heavy to lift alone, so I looked around for some help. We could afford her. My pension from the City along with Jeff's disability checks gave us the wherewithal to buy this two-bedroom frame house with a sunporch in back that I enclosed and plumbed for a second bathroom while I was at it, and installed baseboard heaters we turn on in the winter. My son gets restless in his bedroom and wants to look out the big windows in back if it's too cold to sit on the front porch. No matter what the season is, he doesn't like to be closed up very long in one spot. Anyway, pooling our two incomes, we had enough to hire some help.

When she interviewed, she gave us a good impression. Her dark slacks and ironed blouse were neat and clean. Jeff liked her right away. I'd say she was in her early forties at the time. Recently she told me she's forty-eight. With the interview being roughly six years ago, I'd say my guess was about right.

"Myrtle?" Jeff asked me just now. He has trouble speaking, but Myrtle and I understand him. You just have to slow down and listen.

"She'll be late today," I said. "Her niece is graduating from high school." Across the street, three boys were jumping the curb and tossing their bikes onto the grass. If they stayed at the playground for a while, he'd be too busy watching them to think about Myrtle's change in schedule. He gets restless when things change. You have to give him a heads-up before it's time for meals or bedtime. Change is hard for me, too. I like to know ahead of time what I'm going to be doing. What's expected of me.

I would have liked a heads-up before Jeff's mother left the two of us to live by ourselves.

"Do you want a peanut butter sandwich for lunch?" I asked. "Or how about grilled cheese?"

"Cheese," he said without looking away from the boys. I cleared his 11:00 a.m. medications off the porch and went in to start making lunch. I heard him laughing, an infectious gurgle that makes you smile when you hear it. When I went out with napkins and silverware and Jeff's Coke, I saw the dog, a big yellow dog of mixed breed, across the street, resting on the cement pad next to the picnic table.

"Big dog," Jeff said, pointing with the finger he can control. The boys had gone over to pet him. They were looking for a collar buried in the thick fur, then bent down to look for a tag. Two of them worked in front while the third boy was trying to lift the rear.

"Big dog," I said. Finally they gave up and went back to the jungle gym they were too old for.

When I came out with lunch, the dog was gone. The boys were gone, too. Jeff lost interest until we saw the dog come up the grassy rise behind the picnic table and let himself down in the same spot as before, resting on his front legs with his paws lined up in front of him.

"That dog is old," I said.

"Find owner," Jeff said.

"Maybe I'll go over after lunch."

"Now," said Jeff.

"My grilled cheese will get cold," I said.

"After cheese," he said. I ate my sandwich and drank some beer before I took the porch steps down to the side-walk and crossed the street. The dog was old, all right. The hair around his eyes was white and bristling. When I got to him, he rolled over to the side for a belly rub. Like the boys, I tried to read the tag. There was a phone number. I put one finger around the collar. Pulling on it didn't get me anywhere. The dog didn't want to get up, and I wasn't going to lift him.

Once when Myrtle first came, Jeff saw a teenage boy standing on the cement slab, not dressed warm enough. We watched him pull his arms out of the sleeves and hug himself under his sweatshirt. The hood was pulled up and tied under his chin with a drawstring. He just stood there leaning against the table.

"He's waiting for his ride," I said.

"Cold," said Jeff.

"He'll figure it out," I said. "He'll start walking if he gets cold enough." But he didn't start walking. Jeff kept staring through the living room window.

"I'll go see what he's doing," said Myrtle—we called her Mrs. Jensen then—when she came in from the kitchen.

"He's old enough to figure out something," I said.

Jeff's gray eyes were troubled.

"He has a cellphone," I said. The boy was in that posture everyone seems to have these days, bent over the phone in his hand. "He can call someone."

Without asking, Myrtle went for her coat in the front closet and walked across the street. I went to the kitchen for a cup of coffee. When I came back to the window, she was already talking to the boy. I've since learned she's a little too prone to help others. When she came back, she didn't take her coat off but opened the closet door and lifted her purse down from the hook. "I'm going to give him a ride."

"Where?" said Jeff.

"He lives out at the edge of town," she said. "You want to go with me?"

"Go with," Jeff said, sitting straighter in his chair. Myrtle looked at me. Jeff and I have learned how she tilts her head and puts her palms together when she wants to make a point.

"Okay," I said. She is a good driver, and Jeff knows how to ride the ramp up into the van without tipping over. They drove the stranded boy home. When Jeff came back he was energetic and happy.

"Home!" he said.

"You got him home?" I said.

"Home!" he yelled. Myrtle hung up her coat and purse and went back to the kitchen. A little later I found her doing laundry on the enclosed back porch.

"Thank you," I said. I knew that, myself, I wouldn't have gone to the trouble of driving the boy home.

"The two of them got along," she said, putting a load of wet clothes in the dryer. "They're both nice kids." My legs went weak. I don't think of Jeff as handicapped and I don't feel sorry for him. He was given the physical condition he has. We were given the family that we are. His mother couldn't live with her disappointment. It would have helped if she'd given me some warning she was going to leave.

But when Myrtle called Jeff and the boy in the park nice kids, I knew how much I wanted him to be regular. I sat down on a folding chair next to the dryer. She was watching me. "You all right, Mr. Tenet?"

I nodded. "Call me Tom," I said.

"If you want, you can call me Myrtle." Ever since, that's what we've done.

*** ***

The old dog finally decided to stand up. I bent down and took him by the collar. He let me pull him across the street, up onto the porch, and over to Jeff.

"Good dog," Jeff said, petting him and ruffling the fur on his neck. "Good dog." I called the phone number on the dog's tag. No one answered. There wasn't a voicemail for me to leave a message.

An hour later when Myrtle climbed the porch from where she'd parked in the driveway, she was still dressed up from her niece's graduation.

"Pretty," Jeff said. "You're pretty."

Myrtle smiled. "I don't usually dress up." She looked at the dog lying quietly beside the wheelchair. "Where'd the dog come from?"

Jeff pointed across the street. "Park." Myrtle looked over at me.

Jeff was right. She is pretty. I've wondered how he would feel when he started noticing girls. Could he have a girlfriend? Would a girl be patient with him? He has the physical equipment he needs. He loves some people. Me. Myrtle. Sometimes he asks about his mother. His gray eyes get sad and puzzled when I tell him she loved us but wasn't strong enough to stay.

"Why?"

Those why questions can't be answered, I told him. I don't know why. "How was the graduation?" I asked Myrtle.

"Fine." She went in the kitchen and started a grocery list.

I followed her. "I can cook chicken tonight," I said. She usually leaves before supper. Most days she helps me get Jeff cleaned up before she leaves. That way the two of us can lift him into the shower and back to the chair. I can handle bedtime, changing him into pajamas, sliding him into bed. A neighbor asked me once why I didn't put him in a nursing home situation where they could tend to him professionally.

"He doesn't need to be left behind twice," I said, and that person never asked me again.

Ever since Myrtle came, it doesn't seem like he's been left behind. She understands what he's saying as well as I do. Maybe better. They laugh together at cartoons on TV. When I change the channel to something educational, they're both disappointed. Sometimes they outright laugh at me, like the time I got Jeff ready for the Methodist Church bus to pick him up for Sunday School, only it was Saturday instead of Sunday.

"Saturday!" Jeff roared when Myrtle pointed out my mistake. Myrtle laughed so hard she had to wipe away tears. "Since he's all dressed up," she said, "let's go to Elmo's Cafeteria for lunch." So we did. It was unexpected, but we enjoyed ourselves.

Myrtle put out water and some leftovers in the corner of the porch. After supper I jerry-rigged a leash and walked the dog in the park.

"Well, he's still here," Myrtle said next morning when she climbed the porch steps and saw the dog. "Did you call the phone number again?"

I nodded.

"No owner," Jeff said. Except when he lumbered up for food or water in the corner, the dog pretty much laid on the porch all the time. Jeff wanted him to sleep inside by his bed at night, but I said no. A dog that big doesn't belong inside.

"There's no way to leave a message," I told Myrtle.

"We could call animal control," she said.

Jeff gave a sharp turn of his head and looked at me.

"Son, we can't keep this big dog," I said.

"Keep him!" Jeff wailed.

Myrtle went over and put her hand on his shoulder. "The dog belongs to someone else." She looked over at me. "We could call Animals in Need."

"Our dog," said Jeff.

"Some things aren't ours," I said.

"Ours!" Jeff shouted. I went over to him and he quieted.

Just before lunch, we heard someone in the park calling, "Bruno! Bruno!" I crossed the street and asked the guy if he'd lost a dog.

"Yeah," he said. "A big yellow dog."

"We've got him," I said. "He spent the night with us." The man, who was probably in his thirties, followed me back across the street and up onto the porch where the dog was resting in his regular spot beside Jeff's chair. Jeff dangled his hand down into the dog's fur.

The man smiled. "Bruno doesn't like to stand," he said, "do you, fella?"

Jeff looked fierce. "My dog," he said. The man stared at my son. Myrtle was standing back by the door to the living room.

"This is the dog's owner," I said to Jeff. "Bruno belongs to his owner."

Jeff didn't look too sure of himself when he said, "Mine."

The man looked at Myrtle. "I can come back and get him in a few hours," he said. "That way your son—"

Jeff began to wail. The dog lifted his pointed ears, then lumbered to his feet, front end first, and walked over to his owner.

The man looked at me. "I can bring the dog back to visit the boy," he said. You could tell he didn't know who Jeff belonged to. I'm old for being Jeff's father. Also, the man probably hadn't been around anyone like Jeff and wasn't sure what to do.

"My son understands the situation," I said, and Jeff got the message. Myrtle offered the man some coffee but he said he'd just had some at lunch and he needed to get home. She went over to Jeff and lifted the hand he'd been petting the dog with and put it back in his lap. The man and the dog climbed down the porch steps and crossed the street. He must have parked in the lot because they disappeared behind the grassy rise where the dog originally came from.

Jeff broke the silence with a tantrum. I've seen it many times, an explosion of furious crying. I was sorry Myrtle had to see it. She tried to touch him, talk to him, but these spells make him strong and he pushed her away, almost knocked her to the floor. I ran over to him and pinned his arms from behind. His head thrashed against the headrest. When it was over I was breathing pretty heavy. Myrtle was pale and grave when I let go of him. I sat down on the glider.

Without saying a word, she got her purse and went down the porch steps to her car that she parks to one side of the driveway. That way I can back out around her from where I keep the van and my truck in the double garage.

"Gone," Jeff said when she backed out onto the street and drove away. I sat in the glider, beaten up by the tantrum.

"Myrtle," Jeff said. "Gone." I knew he was waiting for me to say she'd come back, but I couldn't be sure. We sat there a long time. Jeff stared across at the park. I sat on the glider, too beat up to rock, which was the purpose of the glider.

Since I hadn't gone to the grocery store yet, I checked in the kitchen to see what was in the ice box for supper. There was some ground beef. It was too early to fry up patties. We always have potatoes on hand. Myrtle usually makes a salad before she leaves for the day, but I didn't know if she was coming back. I went out to the porch again and sat on the glider. Jeff and I watched cars go by.

"Myrtle?" Jeff said. "Come back?"

"I don't know, Jeff." He was struggling. Restless. Trying to say something. I rocked a little on the glider.

"Gone," he said. "Why?"

"I don't know why," I said. My shoulders felt like they weighed a hundred pounds. After a while I got to my feet. "Let's watch TV." But he made no move to turn his chair and go inside.

"Do you want an early supper?"

He shook his head no. While I was in the kitchen getting a cup of coffee, I heard him squeal. When I got to the
front porch, Myrtle Jensen was standing beside her car
with the back door part way open. I couldn't see around
her into the back seat.

"Dog!" Jeff shouted as she opened the door all the way
and a black-and-white cocker spaniel jumped out.

"I could leave Spots overnight this one time," she said.

"Jeff has to learn he can't always have what he wants,"
I said.

"I think he already knows he can't have what he wants,"
Myrtle said. She never says much about what she thinks,
so I was taken by surprise.

"He wants to be out of that chair," she said. "He wants
to be like other boys."

I was struck dumb. Angry at what she said.

"The fact is, he can't be like other boys," I said. I felt
humiliated. "He never can be."

"I think he knows that, too," Myrtle said.

"Any idea what you can do about it?" I said, and walked
out of the room. Later, when I came back from walking
around the block, she was making supper. I didn't ask
her to. She moved a pot of geraniums from the glassed-in
back porch to the middle of the table. She worked with
what she found in the ice box. Jeff and I weren't used to
baked meatloaf. She slathered ketchup on top that roasted
to a red-brown in the oven. Her mashed potatoes were
smooth. She always makes a good salad. We were used

to her salads and expected them. For dessert, she made bread pudding with raisins.

She got everything set up and left us to eat by ourselves, which we're used to doing.

"Eat with," Jeff said when she was on her way out. She waited for me to say something. I knew what she wanted, for me to agree that Jeff wanted to be like other boys and knew he never would be. I couldn't say it. All I did was slide a chair out from under the table. She understood it was for her.

The meal tasted good. After supper she washed the dishes. I usually wash the dishes. After some TV and his shower, I put Jeff to bed. Spots slept on the floor beside him that night.

Something was on my mind. It was unexpected but I knew what I wanted to say. "It's late. You can stay the night. I'll sleep on the couch."

She agreed. Next morning she made breakfast. I don't make pancakes, so breakfast was different than usual. Better.

Heartland

I sit on two philanthropic boards. I'm okay with one of them because no one wants to be on it, anyway, so I'm guaranteed to hold an office. But the other one, Heartland Family Services, no guarantee. I'm just one more person. No position.

I was leaving the City Municipal Building on my lunch hour last week when I saw three members of the Heartland executive committee walking along Main Street. We're a non-profit organization that supports local people in need. When I joined the board, I had to work hard at understanding homelessness and mental illness, abuse, addiction, things like that, plus what a 501(c)(3) is and how to spell *philanthropic*. Also I gave a lot of money.

Walking along Main Street during my lunch break, I smiled at the three board members who are, as I say, all on the executive committee onto which I have not been invited. They smiled back and turned into Meg's Diner. I followed, half hoping they would invite me to their table. Actually, except for being on the board, we don't have much in common. Years ago when these three men were young, they set up their businesses: insurance, farm equipment supply, and a car wash that has franchises all over the Midwest. All three worked hard and are now rich, whereas I inherited my money from my father. Their lives intertwine in the town and in business whereas mine doesn't.

I'm used to feeling left out. I'm an outsider and often lonely, but truthfully, it's an effort, intertwining with people. Still, I do want them to know who I am. People at work know me. They smile and use my name. We cooperate with each other to keep the City running. My job is modest and boring (I count the meter money that's been collected and send out notices of parking violations), but it passes the time and makes me feel secure because what if the market crashed and I lost everything that Daddy left me? I'd still have my salary, insurance, and small retirement. It all adds up.

But in another way, it's not adding up. Other people's lives seem to be moving forward better than mine: marriages that last a lifetime, children, promotions, positions, executive committee memberships, whereas, except for my husband, Richard, I'm at a standstill. It's true I'm smiled at and said hello to, but then this is a friendly community and people may not always know or even like the people they smile at.

In Meg's Diner I took a table where the three men could see me. Eventually two women joined them, one on the board and one not on the board. They both smiled but immediately forgot I was there. When their meal was over, one of the men, Russ Trowbridge, dropped behind and stopped at my table while the other four lined up at the cash register to pay their bills.

He smiled. "How are you, Desiree?"

"Fine," I said. "How are you? Would you like to sit down?"

"I don't have time, but I wonder if you could come by my office sometime. I was going to call you this afternoon. There's something I'd like to discuss with you."

"I don't have to be back until 1:30," I said. "Would you like me to come now?"

"I could talk to you here," he said, "but I have something to show you and it's back at the office."

Something to show me! After he left I had coffee and pie, paid my bill, and set out after him. His insurance office is two blocks east of the diner. On my way, several people said hello and smiled, but they didn't call me by name. (Sometimes I think the name Desiree is too strange for people to remember. I was named for my mother who was French.) Maybe Russ Trowbridge was going to say that the executive committee members wanted me to join them and was I interested in participating in their deliberations. But why would he need to show me something?

I passed under the sign, *Trowbridge Insurance*, and the receptionist took me right in. Russ stood up from where he was working at his desk and thanked me for coming so promptly because, he said, this is a matter that can't wait. He pointed me to an armchair. "We have a project we'd like to discuss with you," he said, getting down to business. "When I say 'we,' I mean the executive committee."

I leaned back in the soft chair, maybe a little cocky. "What can I do for you?" I said.

"Something that requires generosity," he said. The first thought to cross my mind was that maybe I wasn't being invited onto the executive committee after all. The second thought was that my husband might not like it if I told him I was giving additional money to Heartland Family Services.

"The State is interested in contracting with us to take in a refugee family and help them get established in the community," Russ said.

"Where are they from?" I asked.

"Congo," he said.

"The Congo?"

"They just call it Congo," he said. "We've done everything except sign on the dotted line."

"Where are the Congoans?"

"Congolese," he said, and stood up to hand me a photograph across the desk. "They're in New York right now. It's a big family. As you can see, there's three generations."

I was looking at a mother, father, seven children, and a grandmother. They were black-skinned and dressed in western clothes. The women had scarves on their heads.

"They're clean and well-dressed," I said. "They look better than I expect refugees to look."

"Maybe so," he said.

"Family of ten," I said. "My father came from a big family. Even after typhoid fever, there were still eight kids left."

"They farmed, didn't they?" said Russ.

"Out in the western part of the state, Grimes County," I said. "But Daddy went to France."

"Right," said Russ. "He was an interesting man."

"These Congolese," I said, "can we put them up in the shelter?"

"There's no room right now," said Russ. Heartland Family Services supports a halfway house for people who are enrolled in the State rehabilitation program. I looked at the photograph again. The youngest child, maybe three years old, was leaning against her mother. Though I couldn't see it, I sensed her little arm wrapped around her mother's knee.

"The State doesn't want to pay for their housing," said Russ. "The budget is tight."

"I guess that's where we come in," I said.

Russ nodded. "Private money."

"How much do we need?"

"We don't know yet. The executive committee is meeting with the State on Thursday and we'll have more details then."

The executive committee! "What do you want me to do?" I said.

"You have a history of charitable giving," Russ said. "We're going to negotiate with the State on Thursday, but we need a rough idea of what we can offer."

"So the executive committee has to come up with a number?" I said.

"That's right. By Thursday. In the meantime, do you think you can help?"

I saw that I wasn't going to be invited onto the committee. "Let me think about it." I began to calculate what I could give and what Richard would think about the amount. It's my money, but I like to please him when I can. "Where will the family stay?"

"We'll have to arrange something," Russ said. "Temporarily."

"What else does the State want us to provide?" I said.

Russ shrugged. "Personal expenses. Food costs. That kind of thing."

"Could they eat at the shelter?"

"Maybe. If they cook their own food, they'll need money for groceries."

"Where would they cook?"

"Wherever they're staying, maybe in an apartment. Maybe with a volunteer family."

"Share a kitchen?" I said.

"The details would have to be ironed out," said Russ. I handed back the photograph. We shook hands and I went back to work in the Municipal Building.

At five o'clock I called Richard to see if he needed me to pick up anything in town and he didn't so I walked directly home. The house smelled good when I got there—garlic and onion. I could hear the olive oil spattering. My husband does the cooking and shopping, and I wash the dishes. Richard appreciates living in my home, a roomy, brick house my father bought forty years ago, and since I love being married to Richard, it works out real well. It's a nice change, having a husband who tells me he loves me and shows it. My other husbands lost interest in me, also in my body, and they weren't very affectionate.

After the left-over spaghetti was put away and the dishes were done, I told Richard about the Congolese family that Heartland might be sponsoring and what did he think about it if I donated money over and above what I was already giving. He didn't say too much, but later, when we finished watching a rerun of Renovate Your Home (I'd already added a deck and a family room to my house right after Richard proposed), he turned to me and said, "Where are these Congolese going to live?"

"It hasn't been decided yet," I said.

"How much did you say the State wants?"

"The executive committee won't know until Thursday."

He didn't say much while we walked to the strip mall for ice cream and back home again. After we'd read the paper and watched the late news, he said, "How much are you thinking of giving?"

I weighed what I thought was a good figure, keeping his possible opinion in mind. His opinions matter to me. "Maybe ten thousand," I said. "The children look sweet. They look like a nice family."

He thought for a minute. "Isn't that a little high?" and he leaned forward to touch my hand. Our Lazy-Boy chairs for watching TV are side-by-side. I love his touch.

The next morning I called Russ Trowbridge from my desk in the Municipal Building and told him he could count on me for eight thousand. I felt good about helping the Congolese family. People go to church and sing hymns (I've always liked *Jesus loves the little children, all the children of the world*), but sometimes their ideas about foreigners can be pretty harsh.

"The executive committee has discussed a fundraiser in addition to whatever you donate so that we can build up support for the family," Russ said.

"Is anyone else on the board giving money?"

"Not to any extent," said Russ. "Considering the addiction counselor's salary increase, most feel they've done what they can this year."

"Sure," I said.

That night Richard said to me, "Is anyone else on the board giving money for the Congolese family besides you?"

"Not to any extent," I said. As usual, he didn't react.

"Why aren't they?" he asked me at bedtime.

"I guess they don't have the money right now. That's pretty much what Russ Trowbridge told me."

The next morning Richard spent some time looking out one window, then looking out a different window. I knew what he was thinking.

"Other board members have children and more responsibilities than I do," I said. "That's probably why they're not giving money for the Congolese family."

"Want to go for ice cream?" he asked after dinner and the news. Again, he didn't say much on the way to the mall. After we got back and read the paper, we went to bed. With my other husbands, bed was for sleeping. But Richard knows how to keep us awake.

On Friday, Russ Trowbridge called me at work and said the CEO of Heartland had signed the contract with the

State to support the Congolese family for six months and that we needed to find a landlord willing to work with us.

"You mean give a discount on the rent?" I asked.

"Possibly," said Russ. "And work with us if any disputes occur. After all, this is a brand-new experience for the African family."

"Do they want to be here?" I asked.

"They've been in a resettlement camp," Russ said. "I think they're glad to find a home." It's always been my understanding that refugees love America. But until now, I'd only thought about the family's pleasant appearance in the photograph, how much money I would donate, and what Richard would think. Of course, in the back of my mind was the executive committee and how they ask me for money when what I really want is to be on the committee, too. I don't want to be an outsider for the rest of my life.

That night when I got into bed, I noticed that Richard was lying flat on his back, staring up at the ceiling. Usually he piles up the pillows and reads until I've climbed in beside him.

"What are you thinking about?" I said, lying on my side to face him.

He turned sharply and took my hand. "Do you still want to be on the executive committee, Desiree?"

"Yes, I do," I said.

"Well, tell them you'll give eight-thousand dollars when they ask you onto the committee."

I pulled my hand out of his. "That wouldn't be nice," I said.

"Desiree," he almost snapped, "this is not about being nice."

"I want to help the Congolese family," I said. "And besides, I don't want to bribe my way onto the committee. I want to be asked."

He thought for a minute. "Eight thousand won't be enough," he warned me. "They'll come back for more."

"The State is contributing," I said, "and we're going to have a fundraiser."

Richard pushed my bangs off my forehead. "They'll come back for more," he said again, and looked like he pitied me.

"When I want to, I can say no," I told him.

"You don't want to say no often enough," he said.

I pointed out that I hadn't wanted to say no when he proposed.

"I'm glad," he said, "because you need me."

Russ Trowbridge and I were waiting for the Congolese family to arrive. We'd driven out to the 24/7 filling station on the highway which also serves as the bus station. We waited in Russ's Lincoln because with its temperature controls, leather seats, and roomy interior, it's more comfortable than the bench across from the pumps. The Heartland Family Services van with Del, the handyman, behind the wheel parked beside us just as the Greyhound rolled up. Through the high, tinted windows I could see figures moving in the aisle, reaching up to the racks for luggage. It gave me goosebumps, thinking about how far our refugees were from Africa. We got out of the car and waited for them to step down onto the pavement. Russ took a piece of paper from his inside jacket pocket and practiced under his breath: "Welcome, Mr. and Mrs. Olomide."

When they were all out of the bus, they stood together in a group talking in their language, though I thought I heard something like *oui* and maybe *l'auto* that reminded me of my father who still spoke a little French by the time he'd moved in with me. I would have expected the Congolese to speak an African language.

Russ stepped forward. "Welcome, Mr. and Mrs. Olomide."

Mr. Olomide straightened. "Good afternoon," he said, and extended his hand. "Very indeed pleased." The mother and grandmother didn't look directly at us. The children, running in ages from about three to probably fourteen, stared with large, still eyes. Del slid open the van door and Russ gestured for them to get in while he helped Del load the suitcases—two were tied with rope—into the back.

The parents waited for the grandmother who took a spry step up into the van followed by the seven children, the mother, and then the father. I've never liked that van because the windows are dark and you can't see what's inside. I felt emotional because I couldn't see the family anymore. Even though people always say our town is a good place to live, the Olomides didn't know that, and there were so many changes, maybe not as many changes as they'd already lived through, but there were so many changes ahead. You have a deep feeling you're watching something important happen. That's how I felt about the Olomides: they were bigger than me. Congo was bigger than our town. Africa was bigger than the United States. I'd never had that thought before and it made me feel large and small at the same time.

*** ***

The Four-Leaf Clover Motel out on the highway worked pretty well for a few days. It was built in the '50s and has eight little rough stucco cottages with a small kitchen and bathroom in each one. Every morning Del picked up the Olomides in the Heartland van and took them for groceries and school registrations and job interviews. But by the time the family had stayed five days in the motel, the executive committee had only found one apartment with a landlord willing to take refugees. On the sixth day Russ called me at work.

"Hi, Desiree. We've finally found an apartment for the Olomides."

"Good," I said. "Where is it?"

"Do you know the Pullman Car Lounge?"

"The Pullman Car Lounge!" I said. "By the train tracks?"

"Well, yes," he said. "There's an apartment above the bar."

"It should be called The Cattle Car," I told him. "That's not a proper place for children to live."

"It's the only one we've found," he said.

"They play loud music until late, and drunks stagger around all hours," I said. "They throw up on the train tracks. That's not a proper place for the family."

"It's not the best," said Russ.

"Isn't there something else available?"

"Not that we've found," said Russ. "If we don't rent the apartment above the Pullman Car, we're going to have to locate a volunteer family to house them while

we keep looking. Just temporarily. In the meantime, are you available on short notice to take the three-year-old and her mother to the doctor?"

"Heavens! What's the matter?" I said.

"The mother didn't seem that worried, but the little girl sounds awful. My wife and I took some cough syrup over but when we heard her for ourselves, we felt she should see a doctor."

"Sure," I said. "I have time saved up at work. Which doctor?"

"The clinic on Walnut Street. Two o'clock this afternoon."

Her breathing was noisy when I arrived at the Four-Leaf Clover. The cough was more like a bark. Once we were driving, I watched in the rearview mirror, how she laid in her mother's lap, still and limp. You don't like to see a little child still and limp. It's not natural. The only time she lifted her head was to cough. The mother said something in what I thought was French and I started to realize that she and the doctor might have trouble understanding each other.

Myself, I thought the little girl had the croup or maybe whooping cough. One is more dangerous than the other, but I couldn't remember which. I pulled into the clinic parking lot and left the engine running while I started looking in my purse for Russ's phone number. But the child had a spasm just then and I thought it was more important to get her into the clinic than to talk to Russ about finding someone who knew French.

When the receptionist heard the cough, she came out from behind her sliding glass window and showed us to a smaller waiting room with a cartoon of a sick puppy and a sign that said, "Aw, so sorry you're sick." As we passed a bathroom, Mrs. Olomide motioned that she wanted me to hold her daughter. "Please. Thank you very much," she said.

Merci, I said when I'd taken a chair in the waiting room and reached out to bring the little girl close against me. I couldn't remember the last time I held a young child. She didn't cry. What a brave little person, I thought, as I brushed her hair away from her damp face. She was quiet and hot. I didn't rock her or talk to her, just let her body, so small and helpless, fill my lap and my arms.

"Name?" I said to Mrs. Olomide when she returned from the bathroom and sat down beside me.

"*Nom?*"

"Yes. *Nom,*" I repeated. I wished then that Daddy had spoken more French at home, and that my mother was still alive. So many things get lost through the years. Sometimes I feel like a refugee myself.

"Joseline." She smoothed her daughter's little skirt and let the child stay on my lap. I felt honored. "Joseline," I said, looking down at her. I didn't smile because the child was solemn. Illness feels solemn.

"You?" said the mother. "*Nom?*"

"Desiree," I said.

"Desiree," she repeated with a nice accent, and sat without talking anymore.

After the doctor's appointment I drove to the pharmacy to have the prescription filled. He told me on the way out of the examining room to run a hot shower and keep Joseline in the bathroom to breathe the steam. He said some people thought it didn't help, but he believed in steam. Back at the Four-Leaf Clover, Mrs. Olomide carried Joseline into the motel and I went ahead to turn on the shower as hot as it would go. Mrs. Olomide brought Joseline into the bathroom where I was already sitting on the floor with my back against one wall and my feet between the toilet and sink.

"Give her to me," I said, patting my lap. There was just barely enough room for us to shut the door. I motioned for Mrs. Olomide to close the lid of the toilet and sit down. Joseline half sat, half laid on my lap, and I encouraged her to lay all the way down. She drew her shoulders back. Maybe it expanded her lungs and helped the breathing. She was still coughing and barking.

There was a thin towel hanging from the rack above my head and I reached up for it. Mrs. Olomide watched me roll up the towel. I motioned for her to get another one and I wrapped it around the first towel until the roll was thick. Then I slipped it under Joseline's back to help her arch better.

The front door to the motel room opened and people started flowing in, kids and men chattering. I heard Del's English and Mr. Olomide's French. Someone tried to get in the bathroom.

Mrs. Olomide opened the door a crack and told one of the kids they couldn't come in, but whoever it was sounded like they needed to, and I wondered how we could keep Joseline in with the steam and still let others use the bathroom. While I was thinking about that, Mrs. Olomide stood and stepped to the shower. She looked back at me and shook her head. I didn't understand until she took her wet hand and touched my wrist. The water was cold.

"Their water heater is too small," I said. She didn't know what I meant, although I'm sure she knew more about shortages than I did. She was taking it in stride, but I wasn't.

We pulled up in front of my house. I'd called Richard and he was expecting us. Russ knew where we were, too, and I think Mrs. Olomide knew why we were here. I'll say this: she is a mild-mannered, trusting woman. Considering that it's her precious daughter, she was willing to ride with me wherever I was going.

Richard met us at the door and led us into the bathroom off the downstairs guest room. He started a hot shower and I sat down on the floor with Joseline. This time it was Mrs. Olomide who rolled a towel and slid it under her daughter's back. She lingered over the towel, light blue, thick, and better quality than the ones in the motel. She saw that Joseline was used to me now and she sat down in the chair by the vanity and looked around at the shelving, medicine cabinet, and tub.

After a while I said, "Do you want to see the rest of the house?" I finally remembered the word *maison*. She went to the door and put her hand on the brass knob but didn't turn it.

"*La maison?*" she said. I nodded yes and called for Richard who came to the door. I said maybe Mrs. Olomide would like to see the house. He made a gesture like "after you," and she followed him out, closing the door behind her to keep in the steam.

Joseline was watching my face with those quiet eyes full of trust. Every once in a while she would cough, less of a bark now, I thought. I also thought her breathing was easier and I stroked her little forehead and smoothed her skirt the way her mother did. We sat there looking into each other's faces. Every once in a while I smiled at her and lifted my eyebrows a little just to let her know I was paying attention. She never smiled back, but her face was calm, and if she sometimes looked away at something that caught her interest, like the bright mirror, she always came back and rested in my gaze because she knew I was there watching, and that I was there listening to her breathing.

"They can't find an apartment for the Olomides," I said to Richard over dinner the next day.

He finished chewing his bite of lasagna. "You said there's an apartment above The Pullman Car."

"I guess the Olomides are willing to live there," I said, "but it's not a good place for the children."

After I'd cleared the dishes, Richard brought in the panna cotta and coffee. Richard's parents were from Milan and I love his Italian habits. By the time my father was living with me, he'd forgotten the European touches he'd learned in France. Daddy and I ate without any flair. We drank coffee through the whole meal and our standard dessert was vanilla ice cream.

"They should take the apartment, even if it's above a bar," Richard said.

"It's practically sitting on the train tracks," I said.

"Beggars can't be choosers," said Richard.

"Who says they're beggars?"

He looked surprised. "There's only one or two freight trains a day now," he said after a few more bites.

"That's beside the point," I said. I carried the last of my coffee into the kitchen which I like to do when I wash the dishes. I wasn't ready to tell him my plan.

What I'd said to Russ Trowbridge on the phone that morning was that I wanted the Olomides to move into my house until a suitable apartment could be found.

"Have you thought this through, Desiree?" he said.

"I believe I have," I said. "It won't be forever. Something will turn up."

"Yes, but there's no guarantee when."

"We have a big house," I said. "Bigger than we need."

"Well, it's a generous offer," Russ said. "If you're sure. . ."

"I'm sure I don't want them living above a bar," I said.

"Is your husband on board with this?"

"He will be." And at the time, that's what I thought. I finished the dishes and went into the living room where I sat down in my Lazy-Boy chair. We watched the news, and when it was over, I said, "Richard, this is a big house."

He put the TV on mute.

"I'd like to host the Olomides here for a short while."

He turned off the television altogether.

"Just until an apartment can be found," I said.

"Why can't they stay at the Four-Leaf Clover? They're already there."

"The executive committee says it's costing too much."

"Can't they negotiate a better price?"

"Well," I said, "Del has to drive the van out to the highway at least twice a day. It costs his time, plus gas."

Richard turned away and looked out the window. It was starting to get dark earlier and earlier now. I hadn't given a thought to the potted geraniums and impatiens since this Heartland Family Services business came up. In the warm months Richard takes care of the yard and I'm in charge of the potted plants. We'd been a good team for two or three years by now, but we hadn't dealt with a refugee issue and we both felt the weather changing.

"What about meals?" he said.

"They won't be here long," I said. "We can all eat together."

Richard's eyes narrowed. I've seen the words written in books, eyes narrowed, and it's very true. Eyes do narrow. They can turn into slits when it feels like dust or bits of gravel or something sharp is coming at them. My heart rate picked up when I looked into Richard's narrowed eyes.

"I thought you like my cooking," he said.

"I love your cooking," I said, and reached out for his hand. "They can cook their own food and you and I will eat our food." His hand didn't move in mine. "But I'm sure they'll like your food. Maybe we can eat the same food." He was still looking away.

"It's your house," he finally said. "You can do what you want."

"It's our house, Richard."

"Those are just words," he said, and got out of his chair and went upstairs.

I stayed where I was, watching the TV screen even if it wasn't turned on. I could see that the meals and the kitchen were more important to him than I realized. And yes, the house did belong to me. Daddy left it to me. Richard and I talked about it before we were married and the lawyer wrote up the agreement that way.

Maybe that's one reason my other husbands left me, because of the house. Before Daddy died he lived with me. I'm the first to admit he could be a demanding person. But I felt like I owed a lot to my father, more than to my husbands. Now here I was, happy at last, no pressures from Daddy because he'd died, and yet I was making my husband very unhappy since I wanted to have the Olomides stay with us even just for a few days.

I went upstairs. Richard was reading in his study. We have four bedrooms on the second floor, so we each have our own room plus our bedroom and still one more downstairs for guests. There was plenty of room for the Olomides.

"We don't have to eat with them, Richard," I said, standing in the doorway. I didn't feel welcome to go in his room right now, and I guess he was feeling like he wasn't welcome in my house; that the Olomides were more welcome than he was.

"They'll be cooking in the kitchen," he said. "They won't know where I keep everything. And what will they cook? Goat? Insects? What do Africans eat?"

"Not very much," I said. "That's one reason so many are leaving Africa."

"The Olomides look pretty well fed," he said, pretending to get lost in his book again. But he looked up after a minute. "Why are they here?"

"It's political," I said. "Russ Trowbridge says it's political." I really didn't know, myself. Maybe they'd sided with the wrong people, like I'd sided with Daddy instead of with my husbands.

Within the week Richard packed two suitcases and left. I came home to the empty house and called his name, but the only answer was a note under the sugar bowl: "Dinner's in the refrigerator. I'll be in touch." I sleepwalked through the evening. I'm sure the lasagna was the same as he always makes, but it was like eating ashes.

When the Olomides moved in for what turned out to be longer than expected, six weeks to be exact, I had a lot to think about and I didn't cry very much over Richard. They cooked and always invited me to eat with them. I was surprised at how good their food tasted. Not as good as Richard's, but I liked the lamb and curry and the pieces of fish or meat they wrapped up in leaves and steamed.

And I loved the laughter and chatter in the house. They were musical and they had two instruments that were small enough for them to pack in their suitcases: a wooden box with a stick that tapped out rhythm and something they called a kalimba that played musical notes. They would begin playing, then they'd sing, and eventually they'd dance. I was transported out of my living room to their world. I didn't ever want the music to stop. Espoir and Merveille danced gracefully and the kids danced in what I would call a more western fashion: fast, jiggily. I call it Congo pop. I liked it all because it brought light and movement to my house which had turned complicated and sad for me.

As I say, after a month and a half the Olomides moved to their own apartment, a two-bedroom unit on the south side of town that they were able to pay for with some federal assistance. By then the father, Espoir, had found a job as a custodian with the hospital and Merveille, his wife, cooked in a daycare center.

When they left I missed them so much that I called them one day and invited them to come eat with me and bring the instruments, but they didn't have a car yet and our city bus system shuts down on Sunday afternoons. I offered to pick them up but they said why didn't I just come over to their apartment and have dinner with them, so I did. It was three glorious hours of their food, holding my little Joseline, and listening to African music. After I got home my bed felt emptier and colder than ever and I cried myself to sleep.

Several weeks later Richard showed up at the front door. "Hello, Desiree," he said.

My face went hot and I could hardly speak. "Hello."

"May I come in?"

I opened the door wider without saying anything.

"How have you been?" he said.

"Fine."

"Are the Congolese still here?"

I shook my head no.

"Maybe you wonder where I've been."

My pride kicked in a little and I didn't admit that I cared. He knew I did, though. He knows me very well.

"I bought a house," he said. I was stunned. The words floated in the air, not tacked down to any meaning. I couldn't even get as far as wondering where it was or how big or small or how much it cost.

He stepped into the entry hall. "May I come on in?"

I turned my back and he followed me into the living room where we took seats on opposite ends of the purple sofa I bought when I renovated and redecorated the house.

"Do you want some coffee?" he said. Coffee was the farthest thing from my mind.

"May I make some?" he said. "Do you want any?"

"I guess I do." I listened to his familiar sounds in the kitchen: the china lid to the coffee jar lifting and settling back in place, the water running in the sink, and, before long, the coffeemaker's hiccups. The stream of coffee began trickling and I smelled the familiar smoky scent. I walked into the dining room for cups in the china cabinet. Through the doorway I saw him standing still, staring out the kitchen window at the evergreen tree that grows next to the patio. After I set the cups on the dining room table, I looked at him again. It seemed like he was waiting for me to say something.

"The coffee smells good," I said. He gave a sound between "mm–hmm" and a single note, calm, like music that you know and trust.

"The Olomides are gone," I said after a while.

"Where are they?"

"In an apartment on the south side of town."

"Are they coming back?"

"No."

He brought the coffeepot to the dining room table where I'd already sat down. I watched him over the rim of my cup, not saying anything, just trying to avoid pain.

"I bought the house so that I can control where I live," he said.

"The Olomides are gone," I said.

"I felt like they were going to stay too long."

"They ended up staying six weeks," I said. He didn't say *I told you so*, but he looked like he wanted to.

"They needed a place to live," I said.

There was a long silence. "Would you consider moving into my house?" Richard said.

"Yes," I said, "but now that the Olomides are gone, you could move back here."

He set down his cup. "I like your house," he said.

"It's our house," I said. "I wanted it to be comfortable for you. That's why I renovated it."

"I'm not here because of the house or the renovations," Richard said.

"I didn't know you had enough money to buy your own house," I said.

"You never asked me how much money I have," he said.

"It's none of my business," I said.

"It is if you think I married you because I needed a house and money."

For the second time in less than an hour, I was stunned. I've heard the words *I love you* from my father (probably my mother, too, but I was too young to remember) and from my other husbands. But it's likely I didn't know what *I love you* means. Possibly I didn't think I was lovable.

"Don't you like my house?" I said.

"That's not the point," he said. "I like it but I don't need it." Then he just looked at me. "It's you I like."

Silence.

"Truthfully," he said, "I think you need me. You're not very practical."

I listened.

"Do you understand what I'm saying, Desiree?"

I didn't know how to answer.

"For instance," he said, "has the board asked you to join the executive committee?"

I shook my head no.

"And you've already written the check for eight thousand dollars, haven't you," he said almost sadly.

"I like the Olomides," I said.

"Certainly. But you can like the Olomides and still negotiate for a position on the executive committee."

I looked away from him, out into the kitchen, through the kitchen window, beyond that into the back yard, and even beyond that. Distance broadened and narrowed. What I was looking at was far and also near.

"To tell you the truth," I said, "I've forgotten about the executive committee."

"But it was so important to you."

"The Olomides are more important," I said.

One evening after we'd gone for ice cream and were settling into our Lazy-Boy chairs for the evening news, Richard said, "I'm not sure what to do with my house now that I don't need it anymore."

"You could rent it to the Olomides," I said, "or let them buy it on favorable terms. Their apartment on the south side is too small for all those people."

You could tell by his expression the thought had never occurred to him.

"You still feel responsible for them, don't you," he said after his face settled down.

"I don't feel responsible for them," I said, "but I love them. That's all."

If You Love a Thing

"You drove all the way from California by yourself?" the man asked. She'd found him sitting on a bench in the middle of the University of Montana campus.

Rebecca nodded. When they both stood, he would be short, she was sure of it.

"What route did you take?"

"Sacramento to Reno, Winnemucca, Challis, and here I am in Missoula."

He hadn't looked away yet. His attention, like so many things on this trip, was a new experience. People were usually not interested in what she had to say. She was boring and odd. She'd been boring and odd for fifty years. She knew that. But right now at this bench she was talking to someone who asked questions and then listened. He looked at her, too. Directly. People so often looked away. She understood that she was an embarrassment. She was very tall. And though she ate bread and dessert with every meal, something Mother had always said she must do, she could never put on the weight her height called for. In addition, her hair was bright red, originally natural, but then she'd gotten old. Mother used to color it, but now Rebecca did the job herself, though Mother had died only recently and so she hadn't quite gotten the hang of it yet.

"Did you hit any rainstorms?"

"It was hot and dry. In Nevada, mountains in the distance looked stubbled, like the face of a man who hasn't shaved. Or like a roast ham stuck all over with cloves." It was one of her foolish statements. Try to be sensible, Mother would have said.

The man smiled. The clock in the tower struck five and the green campus resonated all around. Since she wasn't used to happiness, Rebecca stood. "It's time to go," she said abruptly. "Goodbye."

The man stood, too. "Is your family waiting for you?" She'd been right. He was short. She could see the bald spot on top of his head.

"I'm alone," she said.

"Not while you're with me. Would you like to go for coffee?"

Rebecca shook her head no and looked down into the Montana man's blue eyes. She couldn't tell if they were honest or not. "I'm lacking experience."

"It doesn't take much experience to have a cup of coffee." While she was thinking that over he added, "You're probably more experienced than you think you are."

She remembered the fortune-teller, the hitchhiker, and the Chinese professor she'd met so far on her trip across America and agreed with him.

Next day when she crossed the footbridge over the Clark's Fork River she saw him at the same bench.

"How's the traveler?" He was drinking coffee. He'd turned the bench into a home, with thermos, light jacket, and a scuffed old leather briefcase. "Since you won't let me take you to coffee, I've brought the coffee to you." He picked up the dark green thermos, removed the cup, and unscrewed the insulated stopper.

"How did you know I'd be back?"

"I didn't." He poured coffee and handed her the plastic cup. His own was ceramic and had writing on one side: "If you love a thing, let it go." The other side said, "If it doesn't come back to you, hunt down the son of a bitch and kill it." She didn't know if the statement was intended to be funny or not. She ducked her head but lifted it when she remembered the gray roots.

"Do you live in Missoula?" she asked. Idaho and Montana, she'd read, had citizens who wanted to form their own country. She wondered if this man, like his cup, was extreme.

"I've lived on a ranch outside Missoula for twenty years." He sighed like an introverted, melancholy person who is tall and thin rather than the short, loose-necked, loose-bellied person he was.

"Don't you like your ranch?"

"I can't keep up with it," he said. "There's a lot of work."

"Do you do all the work yourself?" She didn't think so. He didn't look like a lean man who works outdoors.

"I did up until five months ago."

"What happened five months ago?"

"I had a heart attack." Her own heart squeezed painfully. Mother had died of a heart attack. Had fallen from the top step four months earlier and rolled to the first landing. Her head of white hair had bounced against the maroon carpet.

The man took the plastic cup from her hands. "You look stricken," he said.

"I am."

He handed back the cup and looked her in the eye. "Drink your coffee," he said. "I'm not going to die today."

Rebecca had intended to leave by Wednesday, but on Friday she found herself still in Missoula.

"Tonight I want to take you to dinner," Raymond—for that was the man's name—said as he gathered his thermos, jacket, and briefcase from the bench. Rebecca accepted the invitation because he'd told her he was an instructor at the Institute for Rangers in the United States Forest Service and she trusted him. "My car is in Parking Lot B." They began walking deeper into the campus, away from the river and footbridge. With one finger Raymond hooked his jacket over his left shoulder. Rebecca carried the thermos. Her straw purse swung from her forearm. He pointed to an old brick building with steep stairways and long, narrow windows. "My second home."

"The bench is your third."

He smiled. He seemed to like her. She was more likeable here than she'd ever been at home on the orchard in the Sacramento Valley.

"When the weather's nice I hold all my student conferences outside," he said. "People usually find me at my bench."

"Is it really yours?" She knew there were endowed chairs. He laughed again. She'd never been this interesting before. She imagined Mother beside her, whispering, "Careful, Becky," and so for a while she stopped talking in order not to undermine the good impression she was making.

They ate dinner at a restaurant downstream from the bridge. She was prepared to pay her share, but Raymond said she was his guest.

"Would you like to see my ranch sometime?" he asked. They'd finished their meal and were standing on the river walk by the restaurant. In the twilight a white-haired man in wet tennis shoes floated down the current of the Clark's Fork in an inner tube.

"No, thank you. I'm leaving tomorrow on my trip across America."

Raymond turned to face her. "I hope you'll come back and visit me."

It was very unusual for someone to want to see her again.

"I doubt that I will," she said. She watched the old man in the inner tube twirl once, then kick hard in the darkening water. The tube straightened out and he continued on downriver. "Why do you want to see me again?"

Raymond's eyes dimmed for a moment, like lights during an electrical storm, then came on again. "You have no pretense," he said. "None at all." He sounded tired.

Rebecca worried about his heart. "Would you like to sit down?"

"No," he said sharply. "My heart surgery was a success. I wouldn't like to sit down." Her own heart locked up, then raced ahead. She turned twice in place. On the second turn he took her hand. "I'm sorry I snapped." He led her to a bench at the edge of the walk. Though he'd just said he wouldn't like to sit down, he sat down. Rebecca did, too.

"I try to forget about my heart trouble," he said. He let go of her hand, plucked the knees of his trousers to loosen them, rested his forearms on his thighs, and leaned toward the river. "I'm lucky to be alive. I know I'm lucky. But I don't feel lucky."

Rebecca looked closely at his collar, neck, and large-lobed ear. She was surprised that such an ordinary-looking man could make her feel so interested. Instead of listening for an imaginary voice, she was paying close attention to a person who was alive.

"My wife died a year ago tomorrow," he said, and took her hand again.

So many people dying! Under the footbridge boys shouted and swung from a rope, the last of the swimmers, the ones whose parents didn't call them in before dark.

"Would you like to walk to my bed-and-breakfast? It's nearby, right on the river. We could sit on the porch for a while."

Raymond agreed. They followed the river walk that led to the Victorian Inn and climbed the eight steps to the porch. Lamplight shone through the screen door. Somewhere inside, a TV was playing. Raymond looked over the railings into both side yards before he took a chair next to Rebecca's. The porch vine stirred in the breeze.

"Where will you be this time tomorrow?" he asked.

"I don't know yet." They watched evening come on and the green river turn black.

"I hope you'll come back to Montana sometime."

"If I do," said Rebecca, "I'll go to your bench."

Raymond moved his porch chair closer and stretched his legs out in front of him. "You know, when we Montanans see something we like—"

"You expect it to come back to you."

"Of course."

"It says so on your cup."

Raymond took his legs off the chair and set his feet back on the porch. "You don't have anything against strong feelings, do you?" He took her hand. Although they could no longer see the water, they sat and listened to its flow. After a while she felt a stab of uncertainty. They weren't talking and she didn't know how long to sit beside someone and hold his hand if he wasn't saying anything. As if he understood, Raymond said goodnight, descended the porch steps, and retraced his route along the Clark's Fork River that murmured musically in the darkness.

The next day Rebecca left Missoula and drove southeast. At sunset the Wyoming sky was full of pink light. She pulled off the highway, got out of her car, and walked along the shoulder. Flat distances stopped by mountains filled her with loneliness, yet the sky poured so much end-of-daylight over her that she felt bathed in hope; hope and despair as mixed and delicious as—as the hot and cold bath water Mother had drawn for her every night of her life. She stood beneath the fluffy, sunset-shot clouds and wept for Mother; for all the baths she would never take again in Mother's long, deep bathtub; for childhood that was gone, though it had lasted longer than most.

Where does time go? She'd heard people say that before: "Where has the time gone?" They always shook their heads. No one knew the answer.

Without warning, panic struck; split her from forehead to navel. Mother dead. She, herself, fifty. And now Raymond in Missoula with heart trouble. Her own heart swelled unreliably, then collapsed and dropped down what felt like an endless stairwell, bouncing erratically on whatever it struck, faster and faster. She ran back to the car and jumped in. Time was change, and change was everywhere. A minute ago she'd been standing on the highway. The clouds overhead had been shaped one way. Now she was inside the car and already they'd blown apart. Already the red sun was sitting on the horizon. With her own eyes, no scientific equipment needed, she watched Earth roll up and cover it.

She drove as fast as she could to the next town and called Raymond at the phone number he'd given her. She was perspiring.

"Hello, this is Rebecca. I met you at the bench on the University of Montana campus."

"Rebecca. You don't have to explain who you are."

"I'm very frightened," she said, and began to hyperventilate.

"What's wrong?"

She struggled against the wild sound Mother so hated during these attacks. "Don't smoke or eat fatty food," she babbled. "Take care of yourself, Raymond. Don't fry your food. You don't fry your food, do you? Don't smoke or eat—"

"Stop!" Raymond shouted into the telephone. She did. His voice slowed her runaway horses. "Where are you, Rebecca?"

She went back to the car and got the map. "Remington, Wyoming." She looked for a street sign. "Fourth and Main."

"You're just over the state line," he said. "Find a motel and call me back."

She did.

"I'll be there as soon as I can," he said. "Wait for me."

Trembling and weak, she went to bed. At three-thirty the next morning she awoke to the sound of a car engine in the parking lot. Barefoot, she ran across the room to the window, peered out between the drapes, and was immediately blinded by headlights. Raymond had come for her. She nestled her blinded face in the crook of her arm. Now that he was here, she didn't want to see him. She liked the idea of Raymond better than Raymond himself. She was sorry she'd called him. All she really wanted was to drive alone across America, feel Mother's presence, and look at the scenery.

The headlights and engine went off. She walked to the middle of her motel room and waited for a knock on the door. It came, not loud, not soft. She knew she shouldn't open the door to a stranger.

"Raymond, is that you?"

"Yes."

She undid both locks but left the little chain in its track. He stared at her through the crack, then grinned. "See? I'm still alive." She couldn't decide whether to let him in or not. He didn't realize that her panic attacks didn't last long.

His grin faded. He looked at his watch, then back at her. "It's three-thirty in the morning," he said. "May I use your bathroom?" She undid the chain.

While she combed her hair she listened to the bathroom sounds and felt—not panic—but grave uneasiness. She heard the toilet flush and said, as he opened the bathroom door and came back into the bedroom, "I can't have a stranger in my room."

He stared at her. "That doesn't fly anymore," he said. "We're not strangers. Just let me sit down for a minute, then I'll get my room."

While he rested at the round table in the corner, Rebecca perched on the end of the bed. The long skirt of the robe that Mother had given her, satin, with her initials embroidered in a scroll pattern just above the breastbone, wanted to part. She had to hold it together with one hand.

Raymond looked at her chest and said, "'R.Q.' I don't believe I know what 'Q' stands for."

"Quint," said Rebecca.

"Rebecca Quint," he said. She was ready to jump out of her skin with this man in her bedroom pronouncing her name.

"I can't talk tonight," she said. He looked tired. He wasn't smiling anymore. "It was nice of you to drive here," she added. "My panic attacks don't last very long. I wouldn't have called you if I'd been in my right mind."

"How long have you experienced these attacks?" he asked. "Just since your mother died?"

"Since I was a girl." She hoped he wasn't going to play psychiatrist. Mother had taken her to every doctor in Chico.

Raymond put his hands on the arms of his chair and rotated his head and shoulders. "I'm tired," he said again. Rebecca would have liked to offer him the bed while she sat up in the chair, but imagining a man in her bed was even more unthinkable than listening to him use her bathroom. "I started driving right after you called."

She should thank him again, but she hadn't actually asked him to come. "Thank you," she said.

"You sounded terrified."

"I have moments of terror that are so real I can't think of a single reason not to be terrified."

"It's been a long time since anyone was personally worried about me," he said slowly, "or called me long distance."

"Are you going to get a room?"

"I called ahead," he said, but seemed in no hurry to leave. He flexed his shoulders and rotated his head again.

"Would you like a drink before you go?"

"Yes," he said. She had tap water in mind, but he picked up the ice bucket and left the room. Rebecca filled a glass and set it on the table. When he returned he drank down the water, filled the glass with ice and a Coke from the vending machine, made a glass for her, and put out two coasters. Rebecca couldn't refuse. She liked Coca-Cola. She liked its peppery effect. She pulled the chair out from the other side of the round table and sat down. They each took a sip and looked up with eyes watery from fatigue and carbonation.

"My wife was a nervous woman," he said. "Anything and everything made her nervous. She was very sensitive to noise, temperature, color, taste, people's accents, people's manners, people's style, people's motives." He looked around the room as if trying to find more items in what Rebecca thought was already a long-enough list. "She was sensitive to everything."

"Was she small-boned?" Rebecca asked.

"Yes."

"Mother was small-boned," said Rebecca. "And nervous. She worried about everything, but she never had a panic attack."

"You don't seem like a nervous woman," observed Raymond.

"No, I'm large. Large-boned," said Rebecca. "My panic attacks are about large things, like life and death and nothingness. Mother worried about little things." They contemplated their glasses beaded with moisture.

"I'm glad you called me," Raymond said.

"It was the panic."

"It's odd," said Raymond, playing with the coaster, "but the one thing that should have worried my wife most of all, didn't."

Rebecca waited.

"She wasn't afraid to die." He closed his eyes. It was hard to tell under the low-watt bulb in the motel lamp, but Rebecca thought the blood drained from his face.

"Raymond," she said, "are you ill?"

"Just tired," he said. "My wife handled her worries well. Anxiety ran in her family. She was aware of it. Sometimes in a worried state she'd just go to bed. Make herself a cup of tea and go to bed, even if it was in the middle of the day."

"What specifically did she worry about?" asked Rebecca.

"The kids. Finances. Lightning striking the house." He took a swallow of Coke. "Our neighbor's barn was struck by lightning. But for the most part her fears were unrealistic. I finally stopped trying to reassure her because it didn't do any good." He stared at his ice cubes.

"You miss her," Rebecca said. Raymond reached out. She touched his hand across the table.

"The body needs comfort," he said.

Rebecca pulled back. She used her body for getting around. That was all. She didn't mind being an adult, at least she hadn't while Mother was alive, but she didn't want all the nonsense that went along with it.

"I don't want to talk about bodies," she said.

Raymond laughed. "We're not going to talk about bodies," he said, "or anything else."

She thought he was looking at the bed. A pang of anxiety stunned her. But he remained where he was and didn't look at the bed anymore. Finally he left. It was four-thirty, the hour of despair and of faith. Despair that night will never end and that Mother, asleep in her bedroom down the hall, will never wake up. Delicious, bittersweet faith that the loneliest hour is also a bridge to morning; that morning will come in spite of all evidence to the contrary; that Mother, or something mother-like, is waiting at the place where first light nibbles at the dark.

Rebecca turned off her light and drew the drape just enough to allow a slit of false daylight in from the parking lot. She dressed, zipped up her suitcase, opened the door, and tip-toed out to her car. She stood for a moment in the parking lot, wishing she could glide away from the motel without getting in the car or turning on the engine. A cool breeze blew her hair that, to anyone watching, shone quite red under the sodium lights.

She opened the driver's door, slid her suitcase over to the passenger's side, got in behind the wheel, closed the door without slamming it, turned on the ignition, rolled forward, and entered the highway that ran through town. She wished Raymond well. She was sorry to leave on the day his wife, a year ago, had died. But staying behind with him was not possible.

The single stoplight on Main Street swayed in the wind above the intersection and was soon behind her. In two minutes she was out of town. She met no one on the ink-black road. No cars approached. The only headlights she saw were in the rearview mirror. She began to think of Mother, cried for a while, slowed considerably, and when the nice little cry was over, wiped her eyes and resumed speed. The headlights in her rearview mirror remained at the same distance. She sped up. The headlights also sped. She slowed. So did the headlights. She drove steadily for a mile, then gunned the engine. Frightened by the sudden noise, the power under the hood of the car, and most of all by the relentless headlights in her rearview mirror, she made a ragged turn and found herself pointed down a dirt road, without lights or engine, hardly breathing, waiting for the throb of the car that had been following her. Its hum drew nearer. She could have screamed at the slow-moving thing. It downshifted, slowed, found her scent, and paused. The trees, telephone poles, and mouth of the dirt road were illuminated by its frightful yellow lights swinging in behind her. Rebecca jumped out of the car and faced Raymond who was walking toward her, backlit, his engine still running behind him.

"You bitch!" He had almost reached her bumper. If she could get to the far side of the car, she could sprint to the highway.

"What kind of secretive person are you?" he shouted.

"You found me," she said in a voice that surprised her. It sounded almost normal. "You didn't go to your motel room."

As soon as she spoke she dashed to the far side of the car. Out of the corner of her eye she saw him streak toward her in a movement that was much too fast for a short, pudgy man with a heart condition. He caught up to her and grabbed her by the arm.

"What do you think you're doing?" he shouted, and whirled her toward him. In a quick, whirling motion of her own she tore loose, reached the highway, and began pounding down the pavement. He was right behind her. They were both panting. With one large foot Rebecca landed on the white line in the center of the highway and stopped abruptly. Raymond stopped, too.

"You said you were going to your room!" Rebecca shouted. She could hear Mother's crisp commands to stop her tantrum but she paid no attention. "You lied to me! You didn't go to your room the way you said you would!"

Raymond lifted his arms, just visible in the pre-dawn light, and danced with fury on the broken white line. "I drove all night to get to you!"

A truck approached. They saw the fierce, wide-set headlights and felt its vibration. They stepped onto the shoulder and were nearly blown off the highway as it passed.

Raymond's spurt of energy faded. "Let's stop at the restaurant ahead," he said tiredly. "If you don't want to talk to me, just drive on by. I won't bother you anymore."

She looked down the road. "You go first."

Separately the two of them drove down the highway. Rebecca kept a distance until Raymond's right turn signal began blinking. As she followed him onto the exit road she realized that Mother had not offered her usual advice in the last few minutes. It was possible, of course, that Mother had no advice to give. That, however, seemed unlikely.

"Raymond," she began, once they were seated in the truck stop, "you've been very nice to drive all this distance." He didn't respond as she had expected, nicely. In fact, there was an angry look in his eyes.

"You were right," he said.

"About what?"

"You don't know anything about the world."

She bristled. "I'm finding out now."

"You haven't found out anything yet, Ms. Quint. But stand by. I am going to instruct you."

"I left Missoula," Rebecca said, "I didn't come back to you, and now you've hunted me down, exactly as it says on your coffee cup." It was interesting, playing with fire.

"With two significant differences." He leaned forward and put his index finger in her face. He didn't shake it. He just held it there. "First, you called me back. And second, I'm not going to kill you. I would like to kill you, but it would be bad for my heart."

Rebecca moved to one side. His finger followed.

"You are obviously a spoiled, selfish woman who expects the world to be a pleasant place, when it was actually your mother who made it a pleasant place. You didn't have the grit to find out the facts on your own."

Rebecca didn't move, not away from his finger, not away from his fiery face and rapid mouth.

"I can see her now, running interference for you, letting you sleep till ten, buying you clothes like that expensive satin bathrobe and these Birkenstocks which cost a fortune—"

Rebecca pulled her feet back and tried to make them small. She felt herself blush from the chest up in that mottled way she hated, partly from shame, largely from dread of what more he was going to say, because, clearly, he was nowhere near being finished. There he was, leaning forward over the table, forgetting his eggs. He was someone on the trail of, if not a hunted thing, an idea, a thought, a philosophy that he was shining onto her life like a flashlight, better yet, a headlamp from one of those Montana trucks that hunters drive. She, of course, did not have to accept anything he said. In fact, she did not have to listen to him at all. While Raymond repositioned himself in order to keep his finger in front of her nose, Mother, who had not addressed her directly in weeks, suddenly spoke.

"Lies, lies, lies," she said. "Get away from this brute as fast as you can, Becky. Listen how he talks about your mother. He never even knew me."

"Mother says—" Rebecca began, but Raymond was not to be stopped.

"—Birkenstocks, I say, that cost a fortune, when you should have been out working so you'd develop a sense of your own ability. Having a family so you'd understand how precious human beings are, how they develop from small bundles of impulses into remarkable people. Instead of committing yourself to a passionate cause or deep reflection, you were out shopping with Mother."

"The man is an idiot," said Mother.

"No, he's not," Rebecca said loudly. "He drove all night through two states to help me."

"Balderdash. He wants sex. Just like your father."

Raymond had fallen silent. He was staring at Rebecca with red, enlarged eyes. "Who are you talking to?"

"Mother," said Rebecca. "I'm defending you."

He sat speechless.

"I know she's dead, but sometimes she still seems very real to me."

"Obviously."

"She doesn't talk to me as much as she used to."

"That's the best thing she's ever done for you." Raymond finished his eggs, slid out of the booth like a younger, slimmer man, and said, "I'm leaving, Ms. Quint. Let me go. If I don't come back to you, hunt me down at my university bench." He bent down and kissed her in the middle of her forehead. "I'll sweep you off your feet. I'll show you what Montana men are made of. You haven't seen anything yet." And he walked out of the restaurant.

Rebecca wanted to follow him. But he was already driving off down the highway. Her car, the only one in the parking lot, shone pink in the sunrise. She slowly climbed in and turned south toward Colorado.

"Rebecca," Mother said softly, "remember to visit Cousin Millie in Denver, then get yourself back to Chico and the orchard where you belong. And by the way, don't ever take up with a strange man again."

"Be quiet," said Rebecca, touching the spot on her forehead where she'd been kissed. "I never liked Cousin Millie, and Raymond is not a strange man." She lowered her window. The early morning air filled her lungs and satisfied every cell in her body because the wind was blowing from the west, from Montana, and because, in spite of everything, Raymond still wanted to see her again.

Pen-and-Ink

The coffee urn by the plate glass window, its steel surface lively in the sunlight, caught Jim's eye. As soon as he sat down he opened his sketch book with a precise, automatic motion that gave him a kind of authority and began to draw.

"Morning, Jim," said Hiram from the next table over.

"Morning," said Jim, whose eye remained on the coffee urn.

"Saw your son at the City Council meeting last night."

Jim's glance firmed up, not because Hiram mentioned Cade, but because pen-and-ink had taken over his attention.

"Ya oughta draw some of them City Council meetings," Hiram said, scooting his chair half a foot to the right so he could face Jim across the coffee shop tables. "Like the courtroom scenes on TV."

Jim had been ignoring Hiram for years. "Action scenes don't work for me," he said. Any one or any thing resting in its own separateness was what worked for Jim.

He was as interested in the morning light and stillness surrounding the coffee urn as he was in the urn itself. Hiram wouldn't understand Jim's attention to the look of sunlit steel or the nature of a plate glass window. Art, to Hiram, was a picture of something happening.

"Hey, Jim, what'd you feed your boy when he was growing up?" Hiram asked. In high school, Cade had been a star athlete. Now he was the youngest mayor in the town's history.

"Home cooking," Jim said. "His mother fed him well." She'd fed her husband well, too. Perhaps too well for Jim's moderate tastes. Happy to sit in a corner drawing, he didn't crave much in the way of food or attention.

"You could sell your art," she'd said off and on before the divorce. "We could use the money and you'd be noticed for your ability."

"You'd have customers, Dad," said his son. "You'd walk down the street and people would know you."

He'd smiled tolerantly. But even as they fed him advice, he was watching the light on their faces, memorizing bones and sockets and individual hairs, sitting quietly in the surge of personalities not his own.

The question—how he'd fathered someone so dynamic—didn't interest him. Neither did the other questions he knew Hiram wanted to ask: why did your wife divorce you? Why, after forty years at Square Deal Hardware, haven't you been promoted?

Jim's wife was baffled, too, then hurt, then infuriated by her husband's refusal to improve the family's prospects. But Jim, satisfied stocking nails and light bulbs, drill bits and sprinkler heads, didn't want to be a manager. His wife and son finally moved to a small house a few blocks away and Jim moved into three rooms above Square Deal. Through the years he paid down her mortgage, kept current on his own rent, and filled countless sketch books with pen-and-ink.

"Hi, Dad," Cade said, sliding into the chair across from his father.

Jim laid down the pen. "Wondered if you'd be in today." Usually crisp and confident, Cade seemed washed out this morning. Jim's eye assessed the stubble of beard. He turned to a fresh page of the sketch book.

"Don't draw me today, Dad."

The only language Jim knew for asking someone about themselves was pen-and-ink, so he sat and studied his son's face. Today it was a new face. He thought about how everyone has a slightly new face every day. Just watch someone who's been away for a week. You'll see all kinds of subtle differences when they get back.

Cade mechanically stirred cream into his coffee. There was discoloration under the eyes. Stunned, stilled, he sat as wordless as his father. Finally, "Amy broke up with me."

Jim removed the cap of the fountain pen, then put it back again. "The City needs a First Lady," he said to his son.

"That's a good one," Cade said sadly.

Jim folded his hands on the table, at loose ends.

"Go ahead and draw me, Dad." Gratefully, Jim uncapped the fountain pen and began the kind of conversation he knew how to engage in: the back-and-forth between scrutiny and art. His pen moved swiftly, stippling in the growth of beard, dark values seeping into white paper.

"She doesn't think we have enough in common," Cade said. "Or that's what she says."

Jim's pen moved rapidly, quick forays into space, drop-dead attacks into the lush paper. "She doesn't know you," he said, "or she'd be satisfied with you." The portrait began to look like Cade.

Several businessmen in dark suits waved to the mayor from where they stood at the coffee urn.

"She's made her decision," Cade said bitterly. Slowly turning his cup this way and that, he said, "Did you ever try to get Mom back?"

"Oh, yeah," said Jim. "I failed, as you can see."

"Mom hates failure."

"Sure," said Jim. It had taken him years to encompass the marriage and divorce in one word: sure.

Hiram, who fell into a shallow sleep this time every morning, stirred like a pet having a dream. He'd once asked Jim why he'd gotten married in the first place.

It was Jacqueline's beauty. Her high facial bones. Perfect hands and feet. Laughter, all melody. And she loved him back. He couldn't believe how she valued his quiet ways. Even now, opening his sketch book, seeing the blank paper, waiting for the hot strike, the spark of art, he remembered the love and pleasure he'd known when he went to bed with his wife.

Cade looked out the window and back again. "How do you live with failure?"

"You learn," said Jim.

"How?"

Jim shrugged. "Day by day," he said. "Pen-and-ink."

"You could sell those drawings," Hiram said, twitching into full wakefulness. "They're good enough to bring in money."

"They're not for sale," said Jim.

"I heard somewhere that Van Gogh never sold a single painting," said Hiram, "and now they sell for millions."

Jim half-listened.

"You need a retail outlet," Hiram continued. When there was no response he leaned forward. "What've you got against retail?"

Cade shot Hiram an irritated glance but Jim said blandly, "I'm no good at selling."

"You sell pliers and wrenches, don't you?"

"Well, I like the smell of hardware," Jim said.

"You have God-given talent," Hiram said, losing interest in a man so different from himself.

"These drawings are for God," Jim said.

Hiram straightened sharply. "Jesus saves."

"Art saves," said Jim.

"That's not standard Sunday School," said Hiram.

"Non-standard," agreed Jim, and stopped talking.

Outside, storm clouds had been gathering, shutting down the light. Rain began flinging itself against the plate glass window. Cade's mother and Amy hurried through the front door. Cade stiffened. "What are they doing here?" Shaking their umbrellas and closing them with a snap, they came toward the two empty chairs pushed half way under the table.

"Coffee?" Jim asked. The women wanted decaf and while Cade went for two cups, Jim invited them to sit.

"Things are getting out of hand," Jacqueline declared. Chair legs scraped against the pine floor. Jim watched how the ceiling light played over her beaded purse.

"It's early in the day for you to be out," he said.

"Amy and Cade need to talk," she said. "I brought her by."

Jim didn't like to draw when his ex-wife was present, so he closed the sketch book and folded his hands. Cade returned with the decaf, silent and uncertain.

"I like to stay in touch," Jacqueline said, glancing side-ways at her son and gesturing vaguely. "I didn't know anything about all this between you and Amy."

Cade set down the cups with studied precision.

"When I called, she was crying," said Jacqueline. Amy, puffy about the eyes, had turned toward the plate glass window that trembled with each wet gust. Jim toyed with the corner of the sketch book. The wish to draw was an insistent pressure, almost as if random lines were strik-ing the insides of his wrists; as if electric, shorted-out cross-hatching singed his fingertips.

"Amy's shy," said Jacqueline. "It's hard for her to say what she means. The situation needs a nudge."

"She can speak for herself," said Cade, though Amy didn't. Talking about her as if she weren't there created strangeness at the table. Facing his mother, Cade finally broke the unnatural silence. "I'm here because I always have coffee with Dad on Saturday mornings," he said. "Why are you here?"

"I'm here because you're my son and I have your best interests at heart!"

"I shouldn't have come," said Amy, pushing herself to a standing position. Fumbling for her umbrella and shoulder bag, she looked like she might not be able to find her way out of the coffee shop.

"I'll walk you to the door," said Cade. They stopped near the window. In spite of his ex-wife's presence, Jim opened his sketch book and began roughing in the two figures leaning toward each other.

"They're good together," Jacqueline said. "They owe it to themselves to work out their problems."

Jim continued to draw.

"Look at them," she said, as if he weren't already looking. "They just need to be patient with each other. Patience is a virtue. I certainly could use more of it, but when there's a way to fix a problem and it's obvious, I don't mind saying what I think. I'm practical. If someone is on the wrong track, I don't mind jumping in and telling them so." She sighed and hung her purse on the back of the chair. "I don't know how to talk to Cade anymore," she said. "I can't be quiet and express myself through art the way you do. I have to talk."

Jim watched Amy and Cade move outside under the canvas awning, its scalloped edges dripping rainwater all around them. He turned to a fresh page.

"Cade doesn't listen to me," Jacqueline continued. "If I want to catch his attention, I have to talk about City Council or something like that."

"You could sit without talking."

"No, I couldn't. Then there would just be silence." As if trying out the experience, she paused for a moment. "Silence isn't enough," she concluded. "Something needs to be happening."

"Something always is," said Jim. He began a fresh drawing: Amy and Cade standing outside under the awning, the drip line defining empty space around them. Jacqueline watched the quick nib of the fountain pen.

"I'm so jealous of you," she whispered fiercely. "You never say anything and yet people pay attention."

"I just watch," he said.

"This breakup is so wrong," she said. "Maybe you can slow things down for them." She retreated into miserable silence. Jim would have liked to say the right thing. He closed the sketch book.

"Cade loves her," Jacqueline continued, "and she loves him. I just want them to realize they love each other." She waited for him to say something. When he didn't, she added, "It's hard to guess what Amy's thinking. She's quiet, like you." Nibbling at a cuticle, she added, "Maybe if you were more decisive. . . "

Jim's mind stalled. Like an engine that won't catch, his thoughts labored, then failed. What did she want him to say? Cade would know. Cade knew how to talk to people. He considered re-opening the sketch book to the pen-and-ink that, limited by the drip line of the awning, hinted at something eventful occurring between the two figures outside. But instead, he simply sat, distracted as one thought nullified the next. When they returned from the sidewalk, Amy looked flushed and her hair shone, even though there was no sunlight coming through the window. Cade looked rested.

"Got 'er all settled?" Hiram called out across the table-tops.

Cade smiled enigmatically. Jacqueline looked up, hungry for information. Her face showed an openness that seemed new to Jim. He turned the page and began to draw her.

"Can't you stay?" she asked Amy, who was still standing.

"Not today." Looking at Cade, she touched her lips and stopped just short of blowing him a kiss. When she'd gone, Jacqueline unhooked the beaded purse and her umbrella from the back of the chair.

"I'll leave you to your coffee," she said. Her ex-husband and son stood when she did. As Cade walked her to the door and held it open for her, there was no time for Jim to capture her peaceful expression. Still, he caught the angle of the head and neck: graceful. Not striving.

Back at the table, Cade watched his father correct lines rendered too fast. Settling back in his chair, he said in a low voice, "It wasn't about whether we have enough in common after all."

Jim continued working.

"Amy worries that she's an introvert and I'm an ex-trovert."

"Oh?" said Jim.

"She thinks she can't keep up with me. Politically, I mean."

"Few can," said his father.

"I asked her what was really bothering her."

Jim paused in his cross-hatching.

"Don't take this wrong, Dad, but she's afraid she's like you and I'm like Mom and that we'd end up getting divorced."

Jim suddenly felt too weak to draw, almost unable to hold the pen. A sense of failure overwhelmed him.

Cade leaned forward and continued. "But even that wasn't what was really bothering her. She doesn't think I listen to her. She wants me to watch and listen. Like you."

"Sometimes that isn't enough," said Jim.

"She mentioned your drawing," said Cade. "She says it's your way of listening."

"I don't know," said Jim, looking at his son with absorbing stillness. "I just draw." He laid down a line or two. "Your mother and I failed."

Cade hesitated. "I think you could get her back, Dad."

"What's done is done," said Jim. "We produced a good son, and that's what's left of us."

Cade looked down, eventually stirring as if to shake off sadness. "Well, yeah, Dad. You have a son. You sure do."

Outside, they said good-bye. The smell of wet sidewalk was in the air. Cade put his hands in his pockets and turned toward City Hall. Tucking his sketch book under his arm, Jim walked at a steady pace, looking closely at everything he passed on his way to the hardware store.

The Creek

"How's this?" Greta stopped the wheelchair near the edge of the creek. The short rainstorm early in the day had blown over. The air almost pulsated with clean woods and sky. Matey's shining eyes darted and settled, moving incessantly from water to trees, rocks to salmonberry bushes.

"How's this?" she repeated.

He nodded blithely. Thumbs up. She was learning how to get around with him. Who would have thought that she could reach Hardscrabble Creek?

It was years since Matey had fished Hardscrabble. He used to park his jeep and put on his waders at this very spot. But the gravel bar on the far side of the stream was new. The water had changed course. Gouging, shoving, it had thrown up rocks and sediment from the creek bed until what had been hidden was now scattered in the sun for anybody to see. Matey knew about undercurrents. He understood the whole creek now.

"—flowers," Greta trilled. God, she was really trilling. "I'm going to pick some Pearly Everlasting. You know those pretty white flowers? Dried? Do you know how they got that way?" she chattered, circling around Matey. "You tie a string around them and hang them upside down. Can you imagine? It must make sap or something go down into the blossoms."

Sap or something. That was as good an explanation as he had. He reached for Greta and touched her hand. You won't find Pearly Everlasting this time of year. You can look but you won't find Pearly Everlasting. You'll find other flowers.

Greta let her hand linger in Matey's. "I'll be back," she said happily. "Are you comfortable?"

Matey made a snappy little circle of his thumb and first finger as Greta darted into the woods.

She'd wheeled him close to the water's edge. The creek was running high this time of year. He remembered dry seasons when logs and trees floating downstream got high-centered on rocks and on each other. They pointed stiffly at the sky or the bank. Brush snagged on the logs and tree roots and dried there, trapped.

But today wood floated and rocks gleamed with wet-ness. He pretended to cast with a sideways motion, the way he used to do when he wanted to lay the line under alders and willows that grew down to the water. His low, sideways casts almost never tangled.

A cut-throat trout took the hook. Matey would reel him in, catching hold of the whipping plump body with its bloody mouth, knocking it in the head with the closed pocketknife, cutting out hooks, washing it, packing it in wet ferns, laying it in the creel.

Greta crashed through the nearest trees, upset. "I can't find any Pearly Everlasting!"

Matey nodded sympathetically.

"All I found were these." She thrust a wild, heavy bouquet of foxglove toward him. "For you," she said. She was out of sorts. She'd expected Pearly Everlasting and the natural cycle was not cooperating.

Matey accepted them with his left hand. He'd never realized how pretty foxglove was. Still holding the long-stemmed flowers, he tilted his face up toward Greta and sought to kiss her. Coloring, she bent down and brushed his lips, then knelt on the ground and hugged him. Matey shifted the flowers and she leaned against his chest. He laid his cheek on the top of her head, and so they sat, feeling the warm sun on their faces and hearing chirps and twitters all around.

"I'll get the folding chair," Greta said after a bit. She went to the van and brought back a striped canvas chair that she set up beside Matey. "Want me to take the flowers?"

Matey handed them to her. She leaned down and laid them on the grass, then kissed him softly, shyly, as she resumed her seat. Matey was surprised. She cares for me.

"Have you fished here before?"

He nodded and showed her his low, side cast.

"I never fished much," Greta said. "Never have been much of an outdoor person."

Matey lifted his eyebrows in a question: What do you like to do?

"Music, mostly. Music and reading. And writing song lyrics."

Matey took out his notebook. "Like your voice."

Greta smiled.

"Sing for me," he wrote.

"My own stuff? I don't write music. Just lyrics."

Matey waited for her to begin. In a quiet, throaty voice Greta sang a few bars:

Love me from afar.
Don't come too near, dear man.
Stay where you are.

Not a very encouraging ditty, Matey thought to himself. Suit yourself. But it's a terrible song.

"I've written a lot of lyrics that never get sung," Greta admitted. She touched his arm lightly. "For years I didn't understand why."

Matey made a question again.

"I tried to write about love and I didn't know what I was talking about." She sat quietly for a few moments. Then, "What do you like to do?"

Matey showed doubt. He tightened and raised a shoulder. He leaned his head to one side and looked into the middle distance.

"You like people." It was a statement. "You understand people."

Yes, I guess I do. He nodded. Some more than others. But yes, you could say that.

"Have you always liked others?"

He shook his head. No. I guess I haven't. "Like people now," he wrote.

Greta dropped her questioning manner. "You are a wonderful man," she said simply. Her gaze rested on him and he responded with an intimate smile. She copied him, unguarded, smitten by their closeness.

He asked her to move nearer. She picked up the long, unwieldy bunch of flowers on the ground and laid them out of the way. Then she lifted her chair and set it up against his.

He gathered strands of her hair that he guessed she'd forced behind her ear in a fit of irritation at not finding the right flowers. He loosened the hair, letting it lie softly against her cheek. The back of his hand trailed across her lips. She kissed his fingers and held his hand for a moment in her own. Matey leveraged himself straighter in his chair. She drew away.

"You've been here many times, I imagine," she said a few moments later, sounding wistful.

Matey nodded. Again he made motions of casting for trout. She smiled. "Caught a lot of fish here, did you?"

Yes. He could talk about fishing and hunting all day. He had lots of stories. Stories about trout and salmon and canvasback and deer and elk. He grinned.

"What?"

But he couldn't tell her about missing the elk when he slipped on the ice. And he couldn't be bothered with writing it down. Damn frustrating, but she didn't need to know everything he'd done.

"Some funny story from the past," she said matter-of-factly. "Well, you'll just have to write it out for me sometime."

Yes. Then he raised his eyebrows and pointed at her.

"Me?"

Matey pulled out his notebook and pencil again. He licked the lead. "Tell about you."

"Well, I've been paralyzed, too." She got to the heart of the matter, this woman. "I've wasted so much time." Her eyes were sad. "I've been bitter. Critical."

"Men?" Matey mouthed.

"What?"

"Men."

"Yes. Men. Everyone." From her chair she bent toward the ground and reached across to the foxglove. She pulled one flower toward her by its stem and said, "I haven't been much of a lover. I've gone through motions." With the stem held between her fingers she looked up at Matey. "Do you think it's too late now?"

Matey shook his head slowly. He laid his hand out flat for her and she took hold of it. Drawing her close, he cupped her head and drew her mouth toward his. They kissed once, pulled apart, then kissed again, not knowing who started and who left off.

He wanted her on his lap, or across his lap. He'd never made love in a wheelchair. He felt like a boy in a car busy figuring out how to shift with the girl close beside him.

God, she'll have to help me. Does she know how?

Greta moved in front of him. She repositioned the foot-rests and parted his legs slightly, kneeling between them.

There she was, in front of him. He could reach her. She stretched up to him and they kissed again. He opened her blouse and gently held her.

"Wonderful man," Greta whispered, covering his moving hand with her own. "My lovely man."

She worked her arms out of her blouse and took off her bra. She slipped back into the blouse and they left it unbuttoned.

Cautiously she moved onto his lap. "Okay?" she whispered. For an answer Matey circled her thighs with his arm and pulled her closer. He smiled, kissed her again, and stretched his hand to stroke both breasts. Greta breathed faster and slipped her hand under his shirt.

She surprised him. She was more passionate than he expected. He felt his slowly building erection. By God, he could still count on it. Old and ill, but by God, he could still count on himself.

He rested his hand tentatively on her skirt. She let it be there. Gently he parted her thighs and laid his hand between them. He moved lightly across the cloth of her dress, slowly, rhythmically, then withdrew.

He worried about his legs and the wheelchair. She would have to help him. She was willing. He was sure of it.

She stood up, buttoning her blouse and tucking it into her skirt.

Matey eased himself where his trousers were too tight. Greta watched. She reached down and held her hand over the hard rise, kissed his mouth, and pulled away. She resumed her seat. They sat holding hands, listening to the water splash over the rocks.

Matey looked at her, touched her hair again. "Love you," he mouthed.

"I love you." Her words came out round and full. Her face was open. He'd made her happy. Suddenly color, sound, Greta herself were almost more than he could bear. He felt a strong, desperate urge to be always this alive.

"Would you consider taking a trip with me?" Greta asked.

Trip? What kind of trip? Matey checked the impulse to say no. He'd taken plenty of trips in his time. He used to travel at the drop of a hat, usually for fish or game. He'd traveled alone. He'd traveled in groups. He'd traveled to see a woman or to leave a woman. But he could not remember ever traveling with a woman.

"I sense a certain reluctance," Greta said wryly. She was hurt.

Matey faced her. He shook his head, at the same time tapping his chair, thumping his useless legs with his left hand.

"You see how I get us around," Greta objected. She gave a toss of her head in the direction of the car. "We could have a wonderful time." Her face glowed. She threw her whole heart into an invitation: "Come to St. Louis for a while." She broke into a phrase: "Meet me in St. Louie, Louie."

St. Louis! My God! Leave his caretakers? Leave Mail River?

"What's to hold you back?" Greta insisted.

What's to hold me back? My health. My caretakers. My life.

No. He shook his head.

Greta maintained, it seemed to him, a stubborn silence.

Well, what does she expect? I can't care for myself. He hit the wheelchair hard with his fist.

Greta's eyes flashed. "The wheelchair is not the problem!"

What is, then? If that's not a problem, what is? He wrote: "If not a problem, what is?"

"I didn't say it wasn't *a* problem," countered Greta. She searched his face. "It's not *the* problem. Know what I mean?"

No. I do not know what you mean.

"I can't explain it," said Greta. She held her back stiffly, her head high. She folded her canvas chair and carried it to the car.

She was very intolerant. His first impression had been right. She was a sharp, critical, bitchy woman. He would stay in Mail River where he belonged, with Martha, soft and kind; with Ben, strong and loyal. His life had nothing to do with some high-strung Eastern woman who came in and started making changes nobody wanted; asking people to do things they couldn't do.

Greta came back from the car and knelt beside him. "I'm sorry," she said. She sounded one-hundred percent sincere.

"Sorry," Matey wrote. "Can't travel."

"Yes you can."

Well shit, we're back where we started.

"Just think about it. Think how we came here to the creek by ourselves. Think how I handle the wheelchair." She brushed her fingers against his cheek with a soft, deft motion. "Think how much you're able to do, Matey."

She was partly right. He wasn't totally helpless.

But she'd have to wash him, get him to the bathroom, serve him his food. Martha and Ben knew how to do everything. They would miss him if he left, even for a little while.

"Your home is here," Greta said. "I imagine you dread to leave home."

She's being tactful. She's not going to say I'm afraid.

He nodded. They looked at each other, studied each other's eyes for a long moment.

"Too old to change," Matey wrote.

"Are you really?"

"I'm not well."

"But are you sick?" Greta suddenly lifted her arms to the trees and the sun. "How do you feel this very moment?"

Matey watched her, listened. Did she really want the burden of him for weeks?

He clutched his pencil. "I have to go to the bathroom," he wrote.

Greta blanched, but only for a moment. "How do we do it?"

She wore a brave expression. Matey's heart accelerated with shocked astonishment. Then he smiled, and smiled some more.

Greta joined him. Her laughter rang out, trilled in the woods, ran up and down the scale.

God, it feels good to laugh. She makes me laugh. I love being with her.

The Long Black Cadillac

"You want me to mourn forever?" her father yelled after her.

"She only died three months ago!" Rebecca shouted back. "Do what you like! I won't be here!"

"Mother spoiled you!" His voice carried down the stairwell and out to the drive where Rebecca had already planted one large foot on the retractable step of her new motor home.

"Stop!" He ran out of the house, his new fiancée teetering on high heels close behind—such ridiculous shoes, Rebecca thought, to wear in orchard country north of Sacramento. She grabbed the chrome handhold beside the door to the motor home, ready to haul herself up and begin her trip across America.

"Come down from there!"

But she hung from the handhold, a fifty-year-old woman swinging above the circular drive like an unsupervised child. Rebecca still expected Mother's long, black Cadillac to come purring up the peach-tree drive and that beautiful woman with white hair and comprehensive make-up lean out the window to cry, "What are you doing, Beck? Come down from that thing and see what I've bought you!"

Rebecca's brother, Tom, strolled out the front door.

"Can't you get her to stay?" their father pleaded.

"I guess she'll stay if she wants to," said Tom.

"What?" Daddy cupped his ear.

"He said she'll stay if she wants to, he guesses," the fiancée repeated. Rebecca waved good-bye with one hand, swung even farther out over the pavement with the other, and let her head roll forward. The fall of dyed red hair, gray at the roots, closed over her face in a parody of a curtain call.

"If you think that's funny!" Daddy cried. He tried to free himself from the fiancée's grip. Slowly, as if moving through water or coming back from the dead, Rebecca lifted one large foot toward her father and the woman beside him. The leg of her walking shorts flapped about her white thigh.

"Let her leave since she wants to go so bad," said the fiancée.

"You can't take a trip across America by yourself," Daddy had said to her one evening when they were eating dinner on the screened-in porch. A light breeze carried the rustling of peach trees through the wire mesh. "You've never been away from home before."

"She went to Girl Scout camp once," Tom said, "in the Sierras."

"That was forty years ago!" Daddy laughed and helped himself to another of the flour tortillas the Mexican cook served every night. "In any case, she shouldn't spend the trust fund on a motor home. Both of you should invest Mother's money."

"It's my money," Rebecca said. "Mother left it to me."

Tom's allergy suddenly flared and he pulled out a large white handkerchief. The only sounds on the porch were the crickets in the orchard and Tom's coughing. Daddy slid his glass of iced tea down the table.

"He can't drink anything during an attack," said Rebecca.

Tom sneezed.

"I don't care what the doctors say. No son of mine is allergic to a peach orchard."

"It's not the peaches," Tom said in a phlegmy voice, eyes streaming.

"It's not the peaches," said Rebecca.

"It's"—Tom was overcome by another fit of coughing.

"It's your fiancée's perfume. It hangs in the air."

Tom went to his room for an antihistamine tablet.

"Perfume!" Daddy leaned forward. "If he's allergic now, why wasn't he allergic when she was his fiancée?"

"It's not the perfume, per se," Rebecca said. "You stole her away from him."

Her father stopped eating. Bugs knocked against the screens and left the wire mesh humming.

"You don't know the first thing about love, Becky," he said softly. Even in the near-dark his eyes penetrated hers. Laid open her whole life. Fifty years spent on one orchard. No experience. For a moment Rebecca heard the pulse of Mother's Cadillac. She rose to her feet.

"Rebecca!" Daddy ordered. "Come back here!"

But when she was climbing the stairs to Tom's quarters, the engine stopped. She took one step and listened, then another, and listened again: the only sound was the pulse of the grandfather clock on the landing. She knocked on her brother's door. He opened it, gaunt and red-eyed.

"Don't suffer so," Rebecca said, beginning to weep quietly. "The fiancée doesn't love Daddy. She doesn't love anyone." They stood there for a while, tall, thin, knock-kneed, absently patting each other's shoulders.

From her handhold Rebecca looked out over the orchard one last time, then pulled herself up into the motor home. She retracted the metal step and slid behind the steering wheel. Through the windshield she saw the fiancée tug at Daddy's sleeve once, twice. But Daddy didn't notice. He was staring off down the drive. Rebecca knew he heard Mother's long black Cadillac, too, and didn't have the courage to wait alone.

The Broom

It was one day before Clara's flight home to New York. She threw a broom in the back of the red pickup truck without explaining why and climbed into the passenger seat.

"Mind if I drive around a little?" she said to Al.

He stopped nursing his toothpick and turned to look at her. "If you wait a minute while I stop by the feed store, I'll drive you wherever you want to go."

She laid her hand on his arm. "It's something I want to do by myself. It's irrational. Just nostalgia." They'd talked about nostalgia the night before. It had bothered both of them to be talking when they'd expected to be making love.

In New York, Clara was considered verbal; here she adopted the local laconic style. "Last night in bed. . ."

"Yup."

". . . do you think we're just tired?"

Al leaned forward and checked both directions before turning onto the dirt road that needed blading since the last hard rain. When he'd finished shifting gears and they were bumping toward Oakley, he leaned back and acted like he'd forgotten what she'd said. She knew he hadn't.

"I'm not tired," he said with a twitch of his right shoulder. "Are you?"

"A little."

"You tired of me?" he said, and looked at the road again.

"No. Are you tired of me?"

"No." The day was beautiful, the blue sky lifting high to make room for the mountains beginning to build here in the plains where Western Kansas steadily rises to erupt in the Rockies a few hours west.

"Do you want me to leave ahead of time?" she asked. She never said "ahead of time" in Manhattan. She must have been pulling words from the part of her mind that had formed when she was learning to talk. She derived comfort from thinking the phrases came directly from her dead mother, etched into a little daughter's impressionable mind, carried forward from Kansas, a legacy.

He reached across and touched her knee. "You mean leave today instead of tomorrow?" The impracticality was obvious. "I'll drop you off"—his forehead lifted a little, not enough to be bad manners, but enough to show he was troubled—"and pick you up on my way back." He knew where she was going. The truck almost stayed in the ruts by itself.

The grain elevator a mile away stood high above the flat wheat and alfalfa fields. So did the steeple of St. Elizabeth of the Plains several miles in the other direction. St. Elizabeth was a German Catholic town. The grain elevator was in the Protestant town, Oakley, where the Methodist and Baptist church were well attended but didn't assert their architecture.

When he turned into her grandparents' abandoned farmyard, she got out and stood on tiptoe to reach the broom in the truck bed.

He smiled. "You planning to sweep the place clean?"

"I guess I'm trying to be a good girl." And that, too, was funny because they both knew she wasn't.

"Watch for snakes," he reminded her, and then the truck was trailing dust out of the yard and turning onto the road close to where the mailbox used to sit.

She lifted her feet high in the weeds. Above her, the disengaged windmill squeaked and rattled, turning in the wind. The windmill and the stone wash house beside it, the rusted round water tank on top, all had been there while the family passed back and forth below, drank from the well, nudged open the wash house door with a foot while holding a bushel basket of laundry. All were gone. The work they'd done to keep the house and farm from dust, grasshoppers, had been ultimately useless.

The door to the wash house was padlocked shut. No more swishing water, soap smells, shavings from gray soap bars, two rinses, sometimes three for fine goods. No more mother and grandmother, sister, sister-in-law, aunt and great-aunt voices. All had gone away while the windmill turned in the wind and the prairie, neither kind nor malevolent, absorbed the sun and rain.

The cyclone cellar had no padlock. Its long wood doors, slanting upward toward what would have been the outer wall of the house, were splintered and worn away at the corners. The location of the kitchen door where she used to step out to meet her grandfather carrying pails of milk from the barn past the windmill, up the cement walk, was now brush. The wild growth was already hot this morning, the scent of earth's sweat released. Insects were busy getting food, skittering and flying, buzzing and humming, eating and being eaten in a green, spicy world.

With difficulty she bent down and opened each heavy door. She pulled up and out. One banged to the ground when she lost control. She stared down into the cement stairwell. Stored air traveled up to her, swelling her passages. She'd opened a grave. Damp dirt smell and scent of sour milk penetrated her. Down there is where the separator had been, where the milk was separated from the cream. That's why her grandfather was bringing the pails to this spot, milk and milk foam sloshing over the edges of the metal buckets.

She went back to the wash house where she'd leaned the broom against a leg of the windmill, and carried it to the cellar by its smooth handle. She treasured the simplicity of brooms, buckets, steps into the earth. She bent toward the threshold, picked up the broom, and began sweeping. Corners caked with dirt had to be dug into, struck again and again with stiff bristles. She progressed down each step, delivering topsoil to the bottom. The sour milk smell climbed the steps and passed her on its way up to the prairie. At the last step she swept the accumulated dirt onto the dirt floor, another layer of time added to the cellar. Down here, shelves lined the walls, but the jelly jars and Mason jars of beans, tomatoes, applesauce, pickles were gone. Gone the milk separator. Gone the little puddles of spilled milk the cats licked up. Gone the cats.

She remained motionless for fifteen minutes, and when she came up again and had closed the cellar doors, she felt better than when she'd gone down there, sweeping.

"Did you clean 'er up?" Al said after she'd dropped the broom in the truck bed again and climbed up into the passenger seat. He was expressionless. His head settled a doubtful notch closer to his lifted shoulder.

She smiled ruefully. "The cyclone cellar steps have never been cleaner. I saw the shelves and the spot where the milk separator sat."

He ground the gears more than he meant to. "Take that broom back to New York with you." She ignored his meaning.

"I want to show you something," he said. When they got to the place he was going, which was uphill, a rare high spot that the glacier had missed, he got out. "We have to walk from here."

They walked up a rocky hillside. The wind blew from Canada. They felt it pass them on its way south. She began to perspire and ran her hand across her forehead, then beneath her blouse where she wiped away sweat under her breasts. They reached the ridge that seemed high because the land below was so flat.

She looked for landmarks. "Can you see the farm?"

He pointed to the north. "Behind that line of cotton-woods."

Directly below them was the country cemetery where her mother, grandparents, two aunts, and an uncle were buried. His relatives were buried there, too. He followed her gaze. "They're all underground," he said. "You want your broom?"

He took a step closer and put his arm around her shoulders. He held her against his generous body. "You go back and take care of your husband," he said. "That's what will clear your mind."

"I grew up here. I have to come see the land and you."

"You take care of your husband," he repeated. "That's what our trouble is."

"He's not my husband," she said.

"Fifteen years. That's a husband."

Words died in her throat. Her world buckled before it fell into place again. He disengaged himself and began climbing down the hill. She looked at the distant line of cottonwoods, the gravestones below, the grain elevators to the south, the Catholic spire on the horizon. She followed him. Everywhere grass and plants constituting crops moved in the wind.

City of Tomorrow

Larry loved working with City government, setting up conventions, purring through Exposition Hall's vastness in a golf cart packed with movers and shakers from business interests all over the Midwest and South. He flung out an arm. "As you can see, we have more square feet of exhibit space than you'll find in any city of comparable size."

"What kind of crowds are you expecting for the show?" asked Ezekiel Tate, CEO of *Home At Last* Hotels. He'd driven in from Oklahoma.

"Thousands," said Larry. "We're going beyond regional. We're going national. We want to show off Ellington's schools, parks, business development, medical center. . ."

"What happened to the deal with Flag 'n Country?" asked Marilyn Bassinger of Bassinger & Daughters Modular Homes. Negotiations with the gun manufacturer finally collapsed, she'd read in the Ellington Daily News.

"No surprise. It was all about money." Larry shrugged. "We couldn't offer a big enough tax incentive." Idling the golf cart for a moment, he added, "You'll have high visibility in Ellington. Like Chub's restaurant. Far Eastern Fusion is already pulling in the crowds."

"We're considering setting up food service right here at the trade show," said Chub Jun.

"You could bring in a model hotel room," Larry said to Sam Tate. He was about to suggest an entire modular home to Marilyn, but, soft-pedaling the salesmanship, he started up the golf cart again. In his imagination he saw booths, graphics, and electronic screens mounted everywhere. The hairs on the back of his neck rose. This was the beginning of a new era for the Visitors and Convention Bureau, for Ellington, for the entire region. The heart of the country was going to be a destination, no longer the sleep-through zone between coasts.

Larry's daughter and son-in-law lived south of the river near Herndonville, the little town where he'd grown up. He put on sunglasses against the disk of sun flattening at the horizon. This section of the river road wound west before turning south again. During summer and fall it was a hard, glaring drive. If he were home in Ellington right now, he'd be mixing himself a Martini, but he was willing to sacrifice a cocktail for the pleasure of seeing Jennifer and John. Organic apple juice was a small price to pay.

"Daddy!" said Jennifer, coming out onto the porch as her father turned off the blacktop onto gravel. He got out of the car, climbed the three porch steps, and opened his arms.

"Hi, Sweetie. How's country life?"

Jennifer rested her head against his sports jacket, then held the screen door open. Inside, he shook hands with his son-in-law while his daughter went for the comfortable sweater always left hanging on its hook. John brought out apple juice and the three sat down in front of the weather report.

"I suppose there's a lot happening in Ellington these days," said Jennifer, turning down the volume.

"As you would expect," Larry said, resting his glass on the broad arm of the chair, "from the City of Tomorrow." While the room slowly settled into absorbing twilight, his vision of Ellington's future floated pleasantly above the faux wood paneling and linoleum floor.

"There'll probably be some work in Exposition Hall for you and Sutton Construction before long," Larry said to John when the broadcast was over.

"Sutton mentioned something about a trade show."

"We'll need walls. Booths. Display supports. It'll be a big show. A lot of build-out." John picked up the remote control and turned off the TV while his father-in-law ticked off materials, costs, and deadlines.

"When's Sutton gonna realize he needs a partner?" Larry asked after Jennifer had left for the kitchen.

"He talks about a partnership," said John, stretching his legs, "but I'm not interested. It's nice to get the occasional paycheck, but Jennifer and I have a farm to run."

Larry didn't think of his daughter and son-in-law as farmers. They raised some chickens, tended a garden, watered a few fruit trees, but that wasn't running a farm.

As long as they were going to live off the land, he'd told them more than once, they should increase their acreage and sell on a large scale. Sure, people drove from Herndonville for eggs and herbs and fresh produce, but there wasn't an adequate population base to support the so-called farm. Not taking him or the future seriously, they smiled tolerantly and listened with little interest.

Years ago, the summer Jennifer graduated from high school, Larry had shouted to his wife, "They've offered her an academic scholarship to Oberlin! She's got lots of ability! She'll be in a great college!"

But Jennifer's mother, without imagination, without foresight, hadn't wanted the girl to leave Herndonville. Decades of arguing finally came to a head and he'd moved to an apartment in Ellington where he was already on the staff of the Visitors and Convention Bureau. His wife moved back in with her parents, and his daughter married her hometown boyfriend who grew a garden and worked part-time as a carpenter. And Jennifer herself? She'd gone to the nearest state college and now she was teaching two classes of remedial English at Herndonville High and helping her husband raise a few chickens and weed the garden. Larry had wanted so much for her.

"A spot is opening up at the Bureau," he said to John when the three had migrated to the kitchen table and were halfway through Jennifer's meatless spaghetti. John nodded politely.

Jennifer spoke up. "What kind of opening?"

"Assistant to the head of publicity."

"That's not up my alley," said John.

Jennifer glanced at her husband before asking, "How much does it pay?"

"Depends on how many hours the person wants to work."

"We could use some extra income," said Jennifer.

"If you're interested, go ahead and apply," said John.

"Maybe a few hours a week," said Jennifer.

Startled by how badly he hoped she would broaden her horizons and apply for the job, Larry said, "Talk to Hank Grisham." By now it was dark. Large drops of rain hesitated at the kitchen windows.

"I'll close up the truck," said John, scraping his chair against the linoleum. "Be right back." They heard the screen door close and his steps cross into the yard.

"You'd like the Bureau," Larry said.

"Does it matter that I'm your daughter? Nepotism or something?"

"Don't think so," said Larry. "You'd be working with Hank in publicity."

When John came back, he brought in weather and a sense of commotion from outside. "It's going to storm," he said. "You'd better stay the night."

"Can't do it," said Larry. "Early appointments tomorrow."

"If we ate an early breakfast, you could drive back in daylight," said Jennifer. But Larry didn't want to spend the night on the farm. Herndonville represented the past, and he was a man who lived in the present and future, which was Ellington. When their pie was finished and the table cleared, Jennifer and John walked him out to the steps. Holding hands, protected from rain by the roofline, they stood on the edge of the porch while he got in his Lincoln and circled around to the county road. Through the windshield wipers he glimpsed the kitchen garden, the enclosure for geese, the stand of sycamore.

Once on the road, with house and mailbox receding through the bleary back window, he felt an unexpected pang for the kids and their acreage. Moving through the bottom lands, his headlights bringing up ditches alive with rain, he fought back the desire to drive on into Herndonville, turn in at the roadhouse, cruise down the main street with its swinging stop light, see the stained-glass windows of the Methodist Church shining through the rain. You could always tell if there was choir practice or an evening service. As a kid, after singing hymns and listening to Bible verses, he would go to the roadhouse where the windows shone as brightly as they did in church, except there wasn't any stained glass.

Winding down a phone call with Marilyn Bassinger of Bassinger & Daughters, who sounded interested in the trade show but hadn't yet committed to moving her modular home plant from Little Rock to Ellington, Larry leaned back in his chair and remembered the day he'd driven her through Exposition Hall. He'd been proud of the diversity in that golf cart, although to the locals who still formed the backbone of the City Council, the cosmopolitan aspect of Ellington's development—the Marilyn Bassingers, female CEOs; the Chub Juns, immigrants; the Sam Tates, African-Americans—had to be minimized. The trick was to play the diversity card to elite newcomers who might be attracted from urban centers where there were universities and artistic shops. The other trick was to attract jobs for the average working guy. Elites coming to be near a college, a medical center, fine restaurants, would give Ellington polish and charm, but Larry knew prosperity needs blue-collar jobs and production plants. He sat for a few minutes, preoccupied. City Council members were mostly pro-development. Still, they restricted the Bureau's budget. He needed a bigger staff.

"Maybe we can pair Jennifer up with 2-R's," Hank Grisham suggested a few weeks after he'd hired her. "She reads a lot, doesn't she?"

"Oh, yeah. Jennifer's a reader, and my son-in-law writes when he's not playing farmer. You want to introduce her to the project?"

"Up to you," said Hank.

"Let's give her a little more time," said Larry. "She's a country girl. Doesn't know much about the city yet."

"Hope you can come to a little dinner I've planned," Larry said to Jennifer and John some time later when he was visiting the farm. "It's business-related."

Jennifer showed interest. John took a swallow of apple juice and listened.

"A fellow named Randall Zubrowski is coming to look over Ellington. We'd like to see him open one of his stores here. Want to help?"

"What kind of store?" said Jennifer.

"Books. A California chain. Ever hear of 2-R's?"

Jennifer's face went blank.

"It stands for Readin' & Writin'," said Larry. John looked skeptical. "I met the guy at a Malls for Tomorrow

convention in Florida. Gave a pitch for Ellington. 'You could spread out from California,' I told him. 'Sweep through Ellington and the Midwest. End up on the East Coast and you'll have a nationwide chain.'" He looked from Jennifer to John and back again. "You two know something about books, right?"

"Well, we like to read. And of course John writes," said Jennifer.

"What are you working on these days?" Larry asked.

John adjusted his long frame to the chair. "Poems."

"What're they about?"

"Love," said John.

"Oh," said Larry. He loved his daughter; that, he knew. His parents and brother, sure. But he wondered if he'd even liked Jennifer's mother, much less loved her. "I always meant to read your book," he said. Jennifer went to the bookcase for *The Laborer in the Vineyard.*

Larry flipped through the pages. Inside the cover was the name of the publisher: Fly-Over Press. He laid the slim volume face-down on the table beside him. The very name brought up exactly what he was trying to avoid: the concept of the Midwest as uninteresting. Not worth paying attention to. Fly-over country.

"John focuses on the Midwest," Jennifer said, guessing her father's thoughts and stressing the value of the book. "These poems are about people in Ellington and Herndonville."

Larry turned the book face-up again. "Are there actual people in here?"

"They're real to me," said John.

"Do you use their true names?"

"Nah," said John. "They're real in the sense that they're human. No specific people."

"You won't recognize any of them," Jennifer assured her father who was absently looking at the front and back covers.

"Your CEO wouldn't be interested in it," John added.

"Why not?"

"Not commercial enough."

Larry opened the book and considered the pen-and-ink drawings scattered throughout. "What kind of books are commercial books, John?"

"Well, where you see the same kind of stuff over and over," said John. "Like in grocery stores and Wal-Mart. My book was printed by a local artist who has his own small press."

"Books are books," Larry said, uncertain about what was commercial and what wasn't. "We think Ellington with its college and general prosperity will be a good market for readers. We're not always going to be fly-over country, you know."

"There's nothing wrong with fly-over country," said John.

"Damn right," said Larry.

But he was mystified. Maybe John resented the commercial success he wasn't experiencing, though he'd never appeared to be a jealous man. Larry didn't know if the guy was a good poet or not. "The airport is expanding," he said, taking a different tack. "Travelers like to read. They buy books at airports. Zubrowski could open a branch in the airport."

"I guess if folks are landing at the airport," John said thoughtfully, "we aren't fly-over country anymore."

"Damn right," Larry said. Jennifer announced dinner. Once they'd sat down and served themselves vegetarian meatloaf and mashed potatoes, Larry asked John when he found time to write.

"Poetry runs through my head all the time," John said, and pulled out his phone. "I write the rough drafts on this baby."

"At night he copies out the draft and works the old-fashioned way," said Jennifer. "Pen and paper."

"This CEO may be too commercial for your poetry, but he sells paper. Even if you don't like the books he stocks, you'd buy paper from him, wouldn't you?"

"Most likely," said John. "Something basic. Plain paper."

Driving home, Larry considered his son-in-law, puzzled by the way John used his time. There were so many ways he could make a better living for Jennifer and himself. Getting off that farm and moving in to Ellington would be a good start.

It was beginning to rain again, drops large enough, hard enough, to be called sleet. He rolled his shoulders and let his head fall first to one side, then the other. To his left, the river moved fast, disturbed. The Chamber of Commerce had a permanent River Committee, of which he was a member. In town, he thought he knew the river, but tonight, away from town, he wasn't so sure. Driving north, he was more aware than usual of the ages-old cut in the earth, the deep crack in the mud containing all that restless water.

The river doesn't think about the future, he thought. Maybe it should.

"Spectacular," said Randall Zubrowski as the first course arrived at the Far Eastern Fusion dinner table: six varieties of sushi served on a boat-shaped teak tray outfitted with three paper sails and a low railing to prevent awkward diners who lost control of their chop sticks from dropping food overboard. He looked around. "This is quite a place."

"You bet," said Larry. "I know the owner well. Chub Jun's opened restaurants in Kansas City and Des Moines." Draining his sake cup, he added, "The next course could be almost anything. Korean. Chinese. Thai. You name it." While Randall and Larry worked their forks and Jennifer probed rolls of rice and seaweed, John manipulated his chopsticks with care. Asian music, silver and gold threads of sound winding through the audio system, gently uncoiled above and between dining tables.

"Your father tells me you and your husband have a farm," Randall said, turning to Jennifer.

"Six acres," she replied.

"Keeps you pretty busy?" he said to John. "Full-time job, I bet."

John smiled.

"In between chores, Jennifer and John are great readers," said Larry. "Always have their noses in a book."

"On my tour this afternoon I didn't see a single book-store," said Randall.

"There's a good second-hand book shop on Maple Street," said John.

"It's not the same thing as a store that sells new books," said Larry. "As I mentioned earlier, the region is ripe for a big, commercial store."

"The anchor space at the mall looked interesting," said Randall. As he talked about the physical requirements for 2-R's, Larry noted the expressionless faces of his daughter and son-in-law. If Jennifer was going to succeed as a publicist, she would have to talk more. Animation is the key to sales. Animation and inner fire. And maybe he shouldn't have invited John to the dinner. His son-in-law was everything that salesmanship—excitement, flattery, exaggeration, calculated emphasis—was not.

"Larry tells me you write," Randall was saying to John. Had he voluntarily said that to Randall? The subject didn't feel safe. In fact, John, by now approaching forty, was beginning to seem less and less safe. The guy's motives were a mystery. Gardening, carpentry, poetry didn't seem to constitute an adult life, especially when you lived in an area ripe for growth. Though Jennifer seemed happy with him, Larry was disappointed in his son-in-law. The man was impractical. Had no interest in making money. No eye for the future.

"Have you considered a coffee bar in the store?" Jennifer was asking. "And maybe a place for readings and presentations?"

Good girl, thought her father.

"By all means," said Randall, "if it looks like Ellington could support the build-outs."

"The second-hand shop has bookshelves on wheels," said John. "When an author comes and reads, you just roll the shelves away from the center of the room and clear a space for seating."

"The second-hand bookstore is very small," said Larry.

"But it's an interesting idea," said Randall.

"I built the shelves myself," said John. "Attached the wheels."

"John's read his poetry there many times," Jennifer contributed. "The wheels were his idea."

"Poetry!" said Randall. "What kind of poetry?"

Larry turned his sake cup around and around. *About love*, he expected John to say.

"Sonnets," John said.

"Sonnets!" exclaimed Randall. "Like Shakespeare? Elizabeth Barrett Browning? I was an English major, you know."

"The sonnet form," John said modestly, working his chopsticks. "I'm not in their league, of course."

"It's too soon to tell," Randall said generously. "Too soon to tell," and leaning over the hot mustard, he began to recite.

> *When I have fears that I may cease to be*
> *Before my pen has gleaned my teeming brain*
> *Before high-pilèd books, in charactery,*
> *Hold like rich garners the full ripened grain—*

Larry, forgetting to eat or drink, noted the deepened pitch of the CEO's voice, the gaze into the middle distance, the slight sway of head and shoulders. Jennifer seemed transfixed.

> *When I behold, upon the night's starred face,*
> *Huge cloudy symbols of a high romance*
> *And think that I may never live to trace*
> *Their shadows with the magic hand of chance;*
> *And when I feel, fair creature of an hour,*
> *That I shall never look upon thee more,*
> *Never have relish in the faery power*
> *Of unreflecting love—*

The two men finished the poem together.

> *—then on the shore*
> *Of the wide world I stand alone, and think*
> *Till love and fame to nothingness do sink.*

"Keats," Randall almost whispered.

Larry pondered this unexpected turn in the meal. He couldn't help admiring the men's poetic leanings. He, himself, was only a salesman. He'd always known who he was, a man with no special talent. He usually knew, though, when something was practical. When something was working. And this dinner was working. John, Randall Zubrowski, and the poetry surprised him, but he recognized that the party had suddenly come alive; burst into flame. He was struck with an insight: the future of Ellington was going to be great. Colorful. The City of Tomorrow was not an idle dream.

As the music of Keats faded, as the glow in his daughter's face returned to its usual steady light, as the sushi was replaced by mu shu pork, Larry said, "I think Jennifer and John can be a liaison between 2-R's and the City of Ellington."

"We'll have to discuss those tax incentives," Zubrowski replied with a wink that included the table, the Far Eastern Fusion wait staff, the entire room, and, it seemed, all of Ellington. Everyone and everything seemed to smile back. John, however, concentrated on his mu shu pork, manipulating chopsticks with his usual care.

"Hank says you don't seem happy at the Bureau," Larry said to his daughter when he was visiting the farm in January. Until now, Hank Grisham hadn't said much about Jennifer's work performance. Larry himself had not seen her display real interest in the Bureau. He'd tiptoed around the subject, hoping he wouldn't have to hear Hank say some morning, "We need to talk about Jennifer."

"I spoke to him yesterday," Jennifer said, toying with her tapioca pudding.

"You haven't given it much time," Larry said.

"I'm not doing the job justice," she said. "To tell you the truth, I'd rather just answer the telephones."

The remark hurt Larry. Was she, after all, wholly her mother's daughter, preferring something easy? Something without a challenge or risk? The two women would hide in this little town for the rest of their lives. The thought made him want to jump in the car and drive like hell back to Ellington, forget the icy roads. His daughter was wasting her life in Herndonville.

He'd thought the night with Randall Zubrowski had shown her the many sides of working at the Bureau.

It wasn't all publicity and tours and making contacts. There was poetry. There was one dynamic personality after another visiting Ellington, collectively interested in providing the region with an appealing array of goods and services.

"I want you to be happy," Larry said to his daughter, "but I was hoping you could stretch a little. Use your abilities in Ellington."

"I'm happy with John," she said, "and John is happy in Herndonville." She looked at her husband who was standing up from the table.

"That's all well and good," Larry continued, ignoring the fact that his son-in-law was leaving the room, "but what about financial stability? Ambition? Improving your prospects?" They both heard the front door open and close.

"You've done well for yourself, Daddy," Jennifer replied. "I admire your ambition, but I guess I'm not made that way."

"Your mother sure as hell isn't."

"This isn't about Mom," Jennifer almost snapped. Larry's heart constricted.

"She's held you back, Jennifer," he stumbled on. "You have gifts. You've always been special. I tried to persuade both of you that you should take that Oberlin scholarship."

"But I'm happy in Herndonville!" Jennifer cried. "Why should I take a scholarship I don't want? Why should I struggle in Ellington? I don't even like publicity!"

Larry took a deep breath. "You don't have to work in publicity," he said. "You don't even have to work at the Bureau. But you should find a job you like in Ellington.

The world is moving away from Herndonville. You're gardening, for God's sake! Teaching a couple of remedial classes! Every once in a while John works for a childhood friend who had the sense to put together a construction company!"

"Stop!" Jennifer shouted. "We like our life!"

Larry stared at streaks of rainwater running down the kitchen window glass. It always seemed to be raining in Herndonville. Jennifer stood to refill their coffee cups. "And I don't see that you're particularly happy in Ellington," she added, her hand shaking with the weight of the pot as she set it down by John's plate with its leftovers.

"Is your mother happy in Herndonville, living in that pathetic little house her folks left her," Larry fired back, "getting by on food stamps and the money I give her—which, by the way, I don't legally have to pay anymore?"

"Daddy," Jennifer said quietly, "she's happier than you are."

They endured a stunned silence. Larry picked up a forkful of spinach and set it down again. "I've devoted myself to making something of Ellington and something of myself!" he said, his voice cracking. "Happiness has nothing to do with it!"

"You are making something of yourself," Jennifer said. "Mother and I are proud of what you're doing in Ellington. But is that all there is? Jobs and money and growth?"

"Is that all there is?" Standing suddenly, he removed his old sweater and headed for the front door. Flinging the sweater onto its hook, he shouted, "Yes, Jennifer! That's all there is!"

She came up behind him, took him by the shoulders, and turned him around to face her. "Come back soon," she said, and kissed him on the cheek. He stepped through the door into darkness. Three steps down and he was in his car, starting the engine, spinning his tires two feet from the porch, shooting past the garden, the geese enclosure, the stand of sycamore, before hitting the bump of pavement separating gravel from the highway to Ellington.

He had no desire to drive in to Herndonville tonight. The ice chunks in the river, the pale moon overhead, went unnoticed. To get back to Ellington on the sleet-slick road was his only thought, not whether his daughter was happy or whether his ex-wife was happy or whether he himself was happy.

It wasn't until he'd passed the halfway point that he began to think about Jennifer. Happiness—a piece of wisdom she hadn't grasped—is beside the point. Improvement is everything. Some day she would wish she and John had not gotten stuck in Herndonville, too old to work their part-time jobs, burdened with a mother who couldn't make ends meet. He saw himself, with his good job and strong connections, keeping them all afloat with a monthly subsidy, the only thing they could count on in a changing world.

Just inside the Ellington city limits he pulled into the parking lot of the Bureau and turned off the ignition. Out here it was dark, but the night crew was at work in the lobby. One by one, lights in the individual offices came on as the cleaners progressed through the building. Staring absently at the windows, he saw Jennifer's darkened room come to life. Bathed in fluorescence, her workspace left him feeling immobilized. He felt as empty as her desk; as incapable of turning the key in the ignition and backing out of his reserved parking spot as he was of spending his life in Herndonville. He turned away from the windows only to see, in his mind's eye, the river in a freezing rain. Roiled. Unknowable.

"How the heck are you?" Larry said jovially. He'd had to wait a few minutes before Randall Zubrowski's secretary transferred the call.

"Good! Good!" said Randall. "How's winter treating you in Ellington?"

"Not too bad," said Larry. "The snowplows are rusting." After some small talk, Randall spoke seriously.

"I meant to call you earlier, Larry, and let you know we're tabling plans for expansion of 2-R's as of the present. Of course, we'll revisit the decision from time to time."

Larry wasn't surprised. He would have heard sooner if Zubrowski wanted to open a store in Ellington. "Well, Randall," he said, "we want you here. I hope you'll stay interested. Keep us posted on any new thoughts. You'd be well treated in Ellington. Well treated and very welcome."

"Thank you, Larry. I truly appreciate that. And tell your outstanding daughter and son-in-law hello for me."

Larry leaned back in his chair, feeling injured. Checking his computer screen, he saw a fresh e-mail from Marilyn Bassinger of Little Rock: Bassinger & Daughters Modular Homes was no longer interested in opening a plant in Ellington or exhibiting at the trade show, but thanks very much for the tax incentive.

He'd felt good about Bassinger & Daughters. The company seemed a likely prospect, actually a better prospect than Randall and his 2-R's. The brilliant conversation of

Zubrowski at dinner, his flair and charisma, had made Larry wonder if Ellington could sustain his interest. Now that his daughter was gone from the Bureau, Jennifer and John's passion for books no longer felt like a recruitment tool he could rely on. He'd lost Zubrowski. He'd lost Bassinger & Daughters. Standing up from his desk, unable to concentrate, his thoughts drifted back to Jennifer and John like a tongue returning again and again to the site of a toothache.

"It's been a while since we've eaten at Rowdy's," Jennifer said as John held the front passenger door open for her.

"It used to be the heart of our social life in Herndonville," said Larry, starting up the car.

"It still is," John said once he was in the back seat.

"They used to have good country ham," Larry said. "I guess you won't be eating ham," he added. "D'you suppose Rowdy's has a vegetarian special?"

Jennifer laughed. "We can ask."

"Give 'em a nudge." People needed nudging, he knew. That was a large part of his job, nudging businesses to settle in Ellington; nudging citizens and the City Council to accept growth. People want growth and prosperity without having to change, and he was here to promote change. The drive to Rowdy's was quiet, with occasional murmurs about how the moist air had sweetened and warmed overnight.

"Beers all around?" Larry asked as they took a table at the back of the roadhouse. While the musicians set up their instruments and tested the sound system, John took out his phone and began working the keypad, perhaps pinning down a line of poetry floating by.

"We miss you at the Bureau," Larry said to his daughter after the mic stopped shrieking. "We lost Randall Zubrowski and 2–R's."

"I'm sorry to hear it," said Jennifer. "I saw Hank in town the other day and he told me."

"It's never dull at the Bureau," Larry said. "Prospects come and go." Turning toward John, he changed the subject. "Writin' a poem?"

John smiled. Another silence. Jennifer swallowed some beer.

"How do you know what to write about?" said Larry.

"He notices things," said Jennifer.

"What kind of things?"

"The weather," said John. Larry noticed the weather, too, but had never thought of writing a poem about it.

"What else?"

"The river."

"I've thought about the river ever since I was a boy," said Larry.

"You've driven the river road for years," said Jennifer.

"That, I have. And fished and canoed and swam in it." The music took over and Larry leaned back in his chair. Jennifer moved closer.

"Herndonville High told us this week that we're merging with the Ellington School District," she said.

This was an unexpected blow. Larry had always known that his youth, centered around Herndonville High, would gradually fade away, but he hadn't realized it would be yanked up and discarded all at once. Sure, it was the past making way for the future, but he hadn't expected it so soon. Vaguely aware of his daughter scuffing her chair through the sawdust until she sat even closer, he roused himself.

"I'm applying for a teaching position in Ellington," she said.

He leaned forward and touched her hand. "Ellington High?"

"Junior high remedial reading," she said. He left his hand close to hers on the table. "Junior High is an age of change," she continued. "I've seen kids achieve a lot once they can read well. I love to see them develop."

"You'll get that job," Larry said, warmed by her touch and the hope that she might have a career in the larger world. "If so," he added a moment later, "you'll be driving the river road more often than I do." He looked over at John and winked. "Even I notice the river. It's always the same, yet somehow always a little different."

"Sounds like a poem," said John.

"Maybe so, maybe so," said Larry. The band took a break. Larry hoisted himself out of his slumped position and said to his son-in-law, "You can tell Scott the trade show build-out isn't going to happen immediately. We've decided to put it off till we can create some momentum."

"Scott's busy these days, anyway," said John.

"Doing what?"

"Attending the Police Academy. He needs another part-time job."

"What about Bassinger Modular Homes and Sam Tate's hotel chain?" asked Jennifer, returning to Bureau business. "Aren't they coming for the trade show?"

"Both a no-go as of this time," Larry said glumly.

"Any prospects right now?" John asked politely.

"Flag 'n Country is back talking to us." He turned to Jennifer. "It's not just growth for growth's sake, honey. Flag 'n Country hires a lot of people. It's jobs we need." Impulsively he added, "The reason you're so proud of the kids you teach is because you know they'll be prepared for the future. And without jobs, there's not much of a future."

"Jobs are part of it," she said.

"What else is there?" said her father.

John stirred in his chair and started to speak, but the waitress in cowboy hat, boots, and very short overalls interrupted to take their orders.

"If you're going to get a decent job, you have to be smart," Larry continued. "Alert. You can't live in a high-growth area and not be able to read."

"Is it growth?" asked John. "Or just money?"

"It's the same thing," Larry said. "Why else do you farm and take carpentry jobs? Why does Scott build and work part-time with the police force?"

Jennifer stepped in. "But money alone doesn't make you wiser or kinder or happier—"

"Prosperity makes people happy," said her father. "Is Randall Zubrowski a happier, better human being because he can recite Keats?"

"Yes, I think he is," said John.

"Randall Zubrowski is happy because he built a successful business and makes money. He's rich because he started a chain store," said Larry, "and he's decided not to come to Ellington because he doesn't think it's a good economic decision." His voice rose. "It will be a long time before you hear Keats recited in an Ellington restaurant again, I can tell you that!"

"You don't have to have money to appreciate Keats," said Jennifer. The conversation stalled.

"Dinner that night at the Far Eastern Fusion was a good experience," John finally broke the muddled silence.

"Oh, yeah. Sure. I agree," said Larry. "Who paid for it?" He answered his own question. "The Visitors and Convention Bureau. Ultimately the taxpayers paid for it, that's who."

John, who had been busy over the keypad, lifted his head. "If Flag 'n Country moves its manufacturing plant here and gets a tax incentive, we're paying for guns."

Larry sucked in his breath. "And hundreds of jobs!"

"And arrests and trials and prisons and emergency rooms busy with gunshot wounds," said John. He laid his cell phone on the table. "It's all about money, not making life better." Ending what for him was an extended monologue, he picked up his cell phone again. Loud, repeated chords from the band, the same three chords throwing themselves out into the roadhouse over and over, silenced further discussion.

Driving back to Ellington, Larry rolled down his window and listened to the river follow him almost all the way into town. Stopping at the Bureau to see if anyone was working late, if lights had been left on, if the locks—no, he thought to himself, I'm not here to check on the lights and locks. I'm here because the Bureau is home—he mentally pictured the tour of Exposition Hall scheduled for the next day: Flag 'n Country out of Missouri, along with Keyboards 'n More, a musical instrument manu-facturer from Nebraska.

Sitting in the car, he suddenly realized this trade show wouldn't need recorded music. Keyboards 'n More could provide the real thing. The hairs on the back of his neck rose as he heard brass, reeds, drums, jazz, classical, country, rock 'n roll echoing through the vastness of Exposition Hall. Throughout the day and night, crowds of excited visitors would gather around the bands and ensembles, their eyes wide, their wallets full. First thing in the morning he'd talk to Morgan Miyamoto, CEO of Keyboards 'n More, and see what they could pull together. This was going to be the biggest, best trade show in the history of Ellington, the region, if not the nation. The future was almost here and he and Ellington were ready for it.

The Jury is Out

Day One: Morning

Opening Statement

I cannot sleep. I cannot relax. I cannot give or receive love. I can only listen, write, and transcribe.

I am a court reporter. I have not always been a court reporter. Once I was a baby without a career. Now I'm an old girl pushing keys on a little machine, performing anti-carpal-tunnel exercises when there's a pause in the flow of words. Every day I listen to liars, truth-tellers, victims, and cheats.

"Madam Reporter, what have you learned from all this?" I ask myself.

"I don't answer questions; remember? I listen to other people testify."

"Perhaps, just once, the reporter ought to answer. Put some testimony of her own on the record."

"But I'm not a witness. I haven't been accused of anything. I'm not a party to a lawsuit. I haven't been sworn."

"But you've been sworn *at*. Just the other day, in fact. At home. By your partner."

"I would rather not think about that right now. You'll excuse me, won't you, while I get back to work?"

Realtime court reporters produce transcripts by writing fast, accurate notes on computerized stenotype machines. The shorthand characters captured on disk are instantly translated into English and appear on all the computer screens in the court or deposition room.

I am used to writing computerized notes, as long as you are the one speaking. I prefer to read instant replay of your testimony rather than my own. For years I have been listening to what you say and I write your words a heartbeat after you pronounce them. Your breath is my professional life. When your attorney wants a certified hard copy the next morning, I read late into the night. Every misplaced comma, every misspelled homonym, every misstroke of the finger must be corrected.

Next morning your knight with briefcase wields the keyboard, scrolling backward and forward through testimony. Opposing counsel and client will also be scanning. They are grouped together at the far end of the table, listening to you as closely as I am, but not as dispassionately. They are waiting to prove you wrong; I am waiting only for your next word.

I have been accused of overworking. My partner, Walter, charges me with living merely to work. Judgment is imminent.

I cannot sleep. I cannot relax. I cannot give or receive love. I can only listen, write, and transcribe.

"Madam Reporter," I say, "since you have forgotten how to do anything else, prepare a realtime transcript. You are the witness. Certified hard copy to be delivered first thing tomorrow morning."

I turn to the stenotype machine, plug the realtime cable into my laptop, and begin.

Direct Examination

"Tell me about your childhood."

I cannot bear this approach, so I object. "Overbroad." I look to the judge for a ruling. And here I run into the first problem. Who is the judge?

I can think of a few judges I would not want to hear my case. The wafflers. The flippant. The deadly serious. Actually, the judge I reported today will do: an elderly man, slim and nimble, who remained good-humored yet firm throughout the motion brought by an attorney who didn't want his client's medical records viewed by the other side.

"Invasion of privacy," the attorney began. "Irrelevant to the matter complained of, as I outlined in my papers, which, Your Honor will recall, cited several cases. I can repeat them if I can just get my briefcase open. You may recall the last time I opened my briefcase in this very courtroom I cut my thumb, which resulted in some medical records of my own since I was remiss in seeking a tetanus shot and developed lockjaw, which, fortunately, was successfully treated. . .”

“Get to the point,” the judge said. “You're running on.” That is the kind of judge I need.

My objection is sustained.

“What is the first thing you remember?”

“A dog named Fatty in a small town in Western Kansas. My mother and I were—”

“That will do. Thank you very much.” I lift my fingers from the stenotype machine and shake them at my sides. I cannot write my own trial. My job is to report disputes between two or more parties. I don't remember ever reporting a lawsuit between one person. A private problem, however, can affect public life: a leak under pressure breaks a pipe, spurts into a building, slowly rises, floods the electrical system. . . Murder, for instance. In Britain, under Anglo-Saxon and Germanic law, wergild, the monetary value of a life, was extracted from the murderer's kindred to pay the victim's kin. . .

“You asked me about my childhood,” I say. “Let me tell you about a lawsuit I once reported. A baby was nearly born. He swam up from the depths and almost surfaced. His mother was severely obese and had a history of miscarriage. The plaintiff parents alleged that, because the obstetric nurses did not place fetal sensors properly, the baby died. Someone must pay a monetary value for the little life.

"Unlike that child, I was born. I do not remember the birth, but I can see by the result that I lived; that it was my turn to surface, just as through the ages — who knows? — I may have sunk again and again before clearing the water and lifting into sunlight.

"Am I avoiding the question?"

"Yes. You're doing everything possible to avoid the question." My lawyer—for that is who he is, this man with colorless hair, pale hands, and a hearing aid—has suddenly materialized and takes over direct examination. "Would you characterize your childhood as happy or unhappy?"

"Happy."

"Were your parents good or bad parents?"

"Good."

"Very good, or just good?"

I have an imbecile for an attorney. The judge frowns.

"My parents were kind to me," I say, "and they expected good behavior, so most of the time I behaved well." Since my attorney seems incapable of it, I will, to use a popular phrase—like other catchy phrases that come into common speech on a high wave, hit the beach, and are used by everyone in imitation of everyone else before returning to the great unused ocean of vocabulary—cut to the chase. "My crisis is not related to childhood."

"What is it related to?"

"Adulthood."

"All right. Let me ask you this: what kind of adulthood are you having?"

"Good. Very good. While I'm working."

"And what percentage of your adulthood is spent working?"

"Great percentage. As great as I can possibly make it."

"Well, how great?"

"Do you want me to count sleep?"

"Do you work while you sleep?"

"Yeah, I'd say I do. My dreams are hard work. Lots of slogging. I also grind my teeth."

My attorney is beginning to look tired.

"Explain to the jury the purpose and importance of your work, as you see it."

Jury! How did a jury slip in here? Sure enough, when I turn my head slightly to the left, I see twelve people seated in two rows in the jury box. They don't look interested and they don't look bored. This gives the trial, my actions, my whole identity, a new seriousness. This surpasses any "realtime" I've known. I feel both larger and smaller than ever before: individually significant when I'm listened to. Unimportant in the long run.

Witnesses come and go, as ephemeral as trendy phrases. I reported one case that resolved itself in the first fifteen minutes of trial when both the plaintiff and defendant watched jurors file into the courtroom and realized strangers would be deciding something they themselves had refused to decide.

"Court reporting is important because" — I scan the jurors for someone I can talk to. I find him, my grandfather: an introspective, tough-minded man who reads his Bible once every day and is quickly bored by small talk — "after I write down testimony, it can't be changed later."

"Is that all?"

"Isn't that enough?" My attorney is supposed to be on my side. Of course, since I am both plaintiff and defendant, he is in an awkward position. "I can keep up with fast talkers in any field: engineers, nurses, plumbers, poets, scientists, computer experts, accountants. I can spell almost anything, tell you whether you're from Boston or New York, Minneapolis or Atlanta. After a few minutes I adapt to your speech, body language, and personality. Sometimes I can tell whether you're lying or not. Within minutes I know if you're a person of manners or an oaf; defensive or open-minded; a mature human being or a jerk."

My attorney is uneasy. The answer is more than he wanted. The judge looks interested; the jury, intrigued. My grandfather listens carefully. He is exactly as I remember him, white hair and beetle brows. His left eye wanders off to one side, as if the view straight ahead may not lead to the truth. He recognizes me. The gulf between us—once generations, now eternity—is respectful.

"We will take our luncheon recess and resume at one o'clock," says the judge, dismissing the jury. Without looking back, Grandfather follows the others out of the jury box. Court staff and spectators remain standing until the last juror has filed out. As soon as the judge turns away from the bench, the courtroom rustles and stirs. His Honor, too, is eager to escape authority. Already he has one arm out of his black robe as he disappears through the private door to his chambers.

Luncheon Recess

My attorney remains at counsel table, reading a law journal. I wander down the hall and onto the front steps of the courthouse.

I haven't chosen my courthouse yet. Wood? Stone? It will be a beautiful old building from the past, perhaps like the architectural gem in Quincey, a Northern California mountain town reached by taking the Feather River Canyon up from the valley floor. If you happen to be driving the canyon at five thirty on a chilly spring morning, you'll see a deep red sunrise, so deep that it is an astonishing purple. The lip of the cliff will give way some day. The sinuous river below attracts you as if it were your own artery. You will eat breakfast in a roadhouse heated by a potbellied stove. When you finally reach the small, classic Plumas County Courthouse, you will be happy.

My attorney brings me a cup of vending machine coffee. Thankfully, the lunch hour is soon over and I can get back to work. I take three gulps and return to the witness box.

Day One: Afternoon

Cross Examination

There is no hyphen in this cross examination. Opposing counsel — who materializes just when I need him — is cross with me, and I am cross with everyone, including my attorney.

"It's true, isn't it, that you didn't become a court reporter until you were forty?"

"True."

"That you walked out on your husband and children shortly before beginning court reporter training?"

"Not true."

"Objection," my attorney says. "Irrelevant. Counsel's use of inflammatory language is inappropriate."

Inappropriate! His facts are plain wrong. He's been talking to — I turn to the jury and find my father, an old man now, too old for a jury; too old for me to resent. He doesn't see me, this kindly-faced man with a round head and the self-importance of a small-town doctor.

"Who did your children live with after your divorce?"

"My ex-husband." My father crosses his arms and looks vindicated. "By agreement. We had joint custody." I have been accused in those very words: *You walked out on your children.* And my father has still more charges. *You remarried badly. You've wasted your life.*

But I didn't walk out, Daddy.

Of course you did, and after all we've done for you. Look at your sister, poor thing, keeping her family together, sacrific-ing... He stops talking, overwhelmed by disappointment. O aggrieved one.

"How many times have you been married?"

"Three. They were all quite nice. Until, of course, they weren't."

"Everything after the word 'three' will be stricken," the judge says. But he speaks mechanically. This case is beginning to bore him. He is uninterested in the distant past. Opposing counsel tries to enliven the proceedings.

"Have you slept with more men than you can count?"

"No. I can count them all." I enjoy the stunned silence in the courtroom. I look at the jury. My grandfather hasn't comprehended the answer: my father is furious and embarrassed. He stands. His face is red and his voice shakes with rage.

"I disqualify myself as juror. I cannot listen to my daughter's testimony." He steps on the feet of other jurors in his hurry to get out of the box.

"Hold on," says the judge. "We have a procedure to follow." But my father pays no attention.

"Sir!" bellows the judge.

My father sees me as I really am.

Finally someone is telling him what to do and he has to listen.

My father the oncologist, my hero for years, the man lodged forever in my heart, is being humiliated. His inadequacy will no longer be hidden. My mother, sister, and I have failed in our duty to keep Daddy looking good in public.

"Dr. ___________" — I don't recognize the family name. This is not realtime. This is surreal-time. Putting myself on trial is not a good idea. I've worked hard to hide my flaws, and here I am, bringing them all out in public. Walter, by charging me with being half-alive, has jeopardized my public reputation and my private sanity.

"Dr. ____________, have you ever served as a juror before?" asks the judge.

"No. I've been too busy."

"Doing what?"

"Saving lives. I'm Dr. _____________, you know."

"Yes, I know."

I open my eyes. Suddenly I want to protect my father from the judge's questions.

"My dad is a good person," I babble from the witness box. "He helps people who have cancer. He saves lives. He gave my sister and me music lessons and a good education. When our mother died he remarried and kept the home together. He needs a lot of love and approval to function. He is easily upset."

The judge strikes his gavel on the bench. "Order in the court!" Except on television, I have never actually seen a judge use his gavel.

"Can you weigh the evidence in this case fairly?" the judge asks.

I speak out of turn. "No, he can't. I don't want Daddy on my jury."

"What you want doesn't matter at the moment, Madam Reporter," the judge says. "You are the one on trial, not your father."

"All right," I say. "After all, he's just one of twelve."

"That's the ticket," the judge says.

"I'll remain on the jury," my father says, "but I'm not just one of twelve. I'm number one. Remember that." The other jurors lift their eyebrows. Several smile. By this time Daddy has re-trampled people's feet and stands once again in front of his chair. The juror next to him reaches up and pulls him down into seat number six. Daddy lands with an unceremonious plop, not quite suitable for a preeminent this and a foremost that. Nevertheless, he is seated. The trial continues.

Redirect Examination

Oh, yes, redirect me. I do so long for redirection. I love Walter. I don't want him to leave me.

My attorney has asked his first question, poor benighted fellow who isn't the least bit clever. I must replace him some day. He's an old friend. We've worked together on many cases, so it will be difficult.

"I believe you were a teacher before becoming a court reporter." He's trying to rehabilitate the witness. God knows I need rehabilitation.

"Yes."

"What did you teach?"

"Special education."

"Children with learning problems?"

"And emotional problems."

"Did you have special training?"

"No. Only a teaching credential. At that time special training wasn't required. I didn't know exactly what I was doing, but"—

"Wait for a question," says the judge.

"Did you know what you were doing?" My attorney is transparent in his ineptitude. I am very fond of him.

"I plunged into teaching with passion and curiosity. By this time my husband and I had two sons. I wanted to understand how a child becomes a person."

"And did you?"

"Not exactly. I learned that, like my children, like my students, I, too, was a child becoming a person. I learned to feel like a child and, for the sake of children, to try and think like an adult. Our school held weekly seminars. A talented psychiatrist helped us foster psychic growth in the children at the same time that we expected them to perform intellectual tasks. It was a very exciting experience. I plunged into the teaching with my whole, chaotic heart; wormed my way into the lives of a few children; lit a fire."

"Object, Your Honor," says opposing counsel who is so much smarter than my own. "Mixed metaphor."

"Overruled."

My attorney squints at his computer screen. He's forgotten the online command again.

"You were saying you wormed your way into these children's lives and lit a bonfire?"

"In spite of my ignorance and inexperience, I had some success. Perhaps it was simply because I cared and the kids knew it. Nothing seemed more important than growth, change, and development, both theirs and mine. The small brick building with trailers for classrooms was my university and my nursery. It redirected me. And the direction was stunning. Shocking. I almost cannot bear to think about the redirection." I am testifying with abandon now. My attorney looks worried by the answer to his own question.

"To what do you attribute the end of the marriage?"

"An omnivorous appetite for experience."

"Are you saying you were bored?"

"Yes, indeed."

"Did you love your husband?"

"Yes. There is no end to my love and admiration for him."

"Do you still love him?"

"I love his memory. He died ten years ago."

My attorney gets a sad, sappy look on his face.

"And he still bores me," I add. The jury flinches. The judge pulls back and studies me for signs of monstrous disregard.

"Well," asks my attorney, too foolish to know that, in addition to being a workaholic, I'm not a nice person at all, "did you gain the experience you wished for?"

"Yes. I had many adventures. I had more pleasure and pain than I expected. And I turned out to be a very different woman than I'd always assumed I was." Unspoken doubts quiver in the silent courtroom. It is at such moments I crave my stenotype machine. It is at such moments I fear the total sum of my life parts. I look at the realtime screen; make a definition or two; rewrite a misstroked brief; inhale the anesthetic of verbatim reporting.

O, God, redirect me. I cannot sleep. I cannot relax. I cannot give or receive love. I can only listen, write, and transcribe.

Recross Examination

Opposing counsel, young, lean, clearheaded, is waiting for my cupcake/muffin attorney to disintegrate into a pile of crumbs before he sweeps aside the leftovers and proves to the judge and jury that I am what I most dread to be: a failed person, buried in work by my own shovel, unloving and unloved. He saunters toward the witness box in his well-tailored suit. With ruthless eyes he pins me to an invisible board where I flutter like a torn butterfly. The man is good-looking if you like butterfly-eaters. He stands perfectly still until all rustling in the courtroom ceases.

"This stunning redirection you speak of — your term, I believe — can you describe it for us? What direction? What was stunning about it?"

"Compound question," objects my attorney. Opposing counsel is confident enough (he's winning, after all) to brush the objection aside like a minor annoyance, a gnat, a fruit fly.

"What new direction did you take?"

I turn toward the jury and look into twenty-four eyes. I roam among those eyes like a hand feeling through a purse for something familiar. My father is studying the ceiling. Grandfather meets my gaze with one eye. Behind him, a woman who might be my aunt pats her tidy, undistinguished brown hair. Here a waitress, there a salesman. I think I see a teacher in the back row, number nine. These are people I pass every day on the street. I know in general what kind of men and women they are, and vice versa.

Is it possible strangers know us best? No motives. Just a little common knowledge about facial expressions, body language, and a random action or two.

"My redirection was away from marriage and toward — a new personality. Nothing less than that. Toward individuality. Risk. Toward the bottom, it turned out, and toward working my way back up."

"What do you mean by 'bottom' and 'up'?" asks opposing counsel.

"I slept around. Being single puzzled and worried me. I made some strange alliances before I developed purposes of my own."

"Did you have fun?"

"Some. Mostly I had excitement. As soon as I was without a husband, I felt adrift. I had never really established myself in my own right. I was ruthless in seeking that right."

"Did you finally establish yourself?"

"After many years, yes. But I was a nervous person. An established nervous person. I paired up with man after man. Only my children, court reporting, and a few friends held steady. Apartments, houses, states, towns, husbands, boyfriends changed. But my stenotype machine didn't change. The ritual of depositions and trials didn't change."

Counsel looks baffled. "Court reporting? That anonymous occupation? Is this the stunning redirection you're talking about?"

I leap to answer. "Yes. That anonymous occupation where the silent recordmaker fills pages and pages with speech; where the lawyers and their clients are all too busy to see how well I know them. Yes. It was a stunning redirection. Not only do I listen and learn. Now, after the shorthand notes are transcribed and certified, I write fiction. Stories. Novels. Essays. I roll experience over and over in my mind. I set characters in predicaments. I paint scenes, invent towns and rooms and meals and children, libraries, weather, moments of revelation."

Opposing counsel steps back. I have surprised him. Good. My attorney is smiling. The judge studies me. I look away from the members of the jury who appear interested in the spontaneous speech. I have stated for myself the course of the last fifteen years. Even my father and grandfather are paying attention. I am exhausted and want the proceedings to end soon.

Day Two: Morning

Continued Recross Examination

It is an early morning in winter. The plain gray air holds a slight yearning, too subtle to be called a premonition of spring, but definitely infusing our town with youngster hope. It is Monday, January 2nd. School and court take up today. Our town is peaceful, stuffed, and ready to get back to work after the holidays.

"Let's tie up a few loose ends," my attorney says, though I doubt he can recognize a loose end, much less tie it up. We're at Meg's Place down the block from the courthouse, preparing for today's continued recross. I haven't been in this particular diner before, but I feel as if I know the owner who stands at the cash register and greets everyone by name. The sounds and smells of a Monday morning are familiar.

"Hi, Meg."

"Hi, Jim."

"How you been, Meg?"

"Fine, Barbara. The usual?"

"Hi, Meg."

"Hi, Joe." Meg's eggs, toast, and hash browns are buttery and basic, plenty of whatever you want, individual attention expected and granted, you deserve what you order, you get what you pay for, and if Meg doesn't cook your eggs the way you like them, she tries again until they're right. In this restaurant there is no yogurt or espresso. Meg doesn't serve dry toast or plastic forks. Meg's Place hasn't changed in forty years. Someone will eventually buy it and remodel.

And I know Meg, herself, though she doesn't know me. I see her every day on the street and in the grocery store. I've seen her on innumerable juries. She is literal-minded and cheerful; believes God helps those who help themselves; holds grudges but drops them if they hurt business.

I break my egg yolk with a corner of toast. "The loosest end of all," I say, "is that we're losing."

"It's too soon to tell."

"I'm going to be crucified today. I'm not sure you appreciate the gravity of our position. If the verdict goes against me I'll have to. . ."

My mild attorney gives me a look that could almost be called penetrating. "You'll have to—what?"

"Ask Walter not to leave me. Promise to work less."

"Anything else?"

"I'll have to love him," I whisper.

He seems taken aback. "What is the purpose of a trial?" he asks me, changing focus.

"To resolve conflict."

"By what means?"

"Question and answer before a judge or jury."

"That's the form. What is the substance?"

Who does my lawyer think he is: Socrates? He's supposed to win my case, not get tangled up in questions about ultimate reality. I want to go back to Walter with a verdict of "not guilty" in my hand, prop it up on the bureau in our bedroom, and point to it whenever he says, "Aren't you coming to bed yet?" My lawyer actually reaches for my hand and holds it platonically.

"Why do we need to be judged publicly?"

"Because whatever we're doing privately isn't working," I answer. He was hoping for something more philosophical. We're here to discuss strategy, but he's not interested in strategy. I really should dismiss him. I look into his eyes and am horrified to discover that my own are filling with tears.

"I don't like these questions," I whisper. "All I know is that Walter wants me to relax and that I prefer being tense. It's my nature. My destiny." To his credit, my attorney does not dip into the paint bucket of glossy mental health platitudes. He does, however, pursue his Socratic questioning, an annoying trait in someone who isn't Socrates.

"Why do you prefer being tense?"

"I'm good at it and it pays well." I shake my tears away.

"Is there any amount of tension you would give up in order to please Walter?"

I object. Where is the judge? I need a ruling on these vague and ambiguous questions. They're irrelevant, too. Impertinent. Personal, certainly. Rude, without a doubt. Look at me. He's made me cry. My toast is soggy. I'll ask for a change in representation. At the very least I'll ask for a new order of toast.

My heart races at the prospect of losing this trial and — admit it — having to say I love you. Facing life with a diminished workload. Worse, facing life without Walter.

"How do you view retirement?" my attorney asks. One of his front teeth is out of alignment.

"With horror." At least he's stopped playing philosopher. I wrestle with him for the offensive, but he's slippery.

"Today's recross will be devastating," I say. "Let's think of a strategy."

"Truth is the best defense," he says, and begins to blur and recede. Meg brings the bill to our table and we split it before he completely disappears. The walk to the courthouse happens outside my imagination and I am on the witness stand again. Opposing counsel is anything but blurry.

"Madam Reporter," he begins, trying to catch me off guard by a respectful greeting. "When is the last time you took a vacation?"

I review the past year, then the past two years. "Do you mean an extended vacation?"

Opposing counsel's nostrils quiver. He's caught the scent of victory. "What do you consider to be an extended vacation?"

"Five days," I say. There is a guffaw in the back of the courtroom.

"When did you last take an extended vacation of five days?"

"I can't recall." I look away from those predatory eyes. I can't remember an extended vacation and I can't re-member an un-extended vacation. I can't remember any vacation at all.

Walter is a witty, fun-loving, creative, artistic, actually frivolous man. He would love to take a vacation with me. "It's only money," he says. Easy for him to say. He doesn't have a fear of deprivation that persists in spite of all evidence to the contrary. If I were a millionaire I would still fear deprivation. And there you have it. If opposing counsel asks the right questions, I will have to admit I feel chronically subtracted from; that working relentlessly keeps my fears at bay; that this is only the first layer of my flawed nature.

But opposing counsel isn't on the right track. The best he can do is question my actions. At a formica booth in Meg's Place, my own wimpy, intuitive attorney opened up the real issue: giving and receiving love. I stare out the fanlight of the beautiful old courtroom window. I can hardly wait for adjournment at the end of the day. I will order a pizza and transcribe at the courthouse until dawn. Fear of love will never overcome me as long as I can scroll down through testimony; apply punctuation; tidy up finger errors; certify another transcript for hard copy. And another. And another.

"Do you anticipate taking a vacation soon?"

I shake my head. Extended or un-extended, with or without Walter, I do not plan a vacation.

"Your Honor," I say, for it has suddenly occurred to me that a trial, by definition, must weigh evidence from the past, "can I be tried for something I may or may not do in the future?"

The judge blinks. "Certainly not. There must be evidence." He drums his fingers on the bench. For once my attorney looks alert.

"Your Honor," he says, "I request a sidebar." The judge nods. I pick up my shorthand machine and walk to the bench.

Sidebar

We keep our backs to the jury. The attorneys speak in low voices.

"The witness is obviously suffering from the effects of overwork," my attorney murmurs. I am furious. I am not suffering effects. But as court reporter, I am entitled to no opinion. I take notes in silence.

"You agree, then, that she is guilty of workaholism?" says opposing counsel.

"Not at all." Although I'm proud of his style, my attorney's meaning baffles me. "Her tension comes not from overwork, but from demands imposed by her future." I lift my fingers from the steno machine. I do not believe this new defense. I do not even understand it.

"She writes fiction," continues my attorney. "She undertakes perhaps more than is wise for one person to undertake."

I do not like the verb undertake. It suggests a burial.

"However, she has no choice. It is her destiny to put words on paper. She cannot whisper words of love into Walter's ear."

Patently untrue. I do not believe it, opposing counsel does not believe it, and the judge does not believe it.

"I wish to introduce Exhibit A," says my attorney.

"Show it to opposing counsel," says the judge.

"I don't have it at the moment."

"Why not?"

"I didn't know I would need it."

"What exhibit?" opposing counsel asks. I have the same question.

"An excerpt from one of her books."

Oh, no.

"Is this a published novel?" asks opposing counsel.

"My client has no published novels. It is in manuscript form."

Opposing counsel suppresses a chortle. I am mortified. Show everyone my work? The work that has been rejected by so many agents and editors? I wink desperately, shake my head, roll my eyes, but my attorney ignores me.

My novels will damn me. They contain me. When they are rejected, I am rejected. If the jury reads me they will surely hand down a verdict of guilty. They will see I am no better at writing novels than I am at loving Walter. Furthermore, it will only prove to them that I do nothing but work; that on the rare occasions when I actually stop transcribing, I simply change desks and write fiction.

The judge speaks to the jury. "We will be in recess until tomorrow morning. The remainder of the day will be taken up with a criminal matter."

My case is set aside until tomorrow. The safety of our town takes precedence over the private lawsuit between myself and myself. See the alleged bank robber in his orange jumpsuit come shuffling into the courtroom, chains clanking. During the preliminary hearing yesterday the district attorney easily convinced the judge that there is sufficient cause to set the case, *People of the State of California, Plaintiff, versus Henry* _________, *Defendant,* for trial. The issue of my character fades into obscurity as our town deals with a man accused of violently taking money that belongs to others.

If my attorney is given the rotating assignment of public defender for this Henry ___________, the accused may have to face up to his character, his destiny, as I am having to do. He will be amazed to discover that his public defender prefers the Socratic method to direct questioning; examines character rather than whereabouts; is more interested in enlightenment than in guilt or innocence.

Day Three: Morning

Very early the next morning we are eating breakfast at Meg's Place again.

"Does any of your writing have the word destiny in it?" my attorney asks. I am busy stirring milk and sugar into my hot cereal. "Have you ever written on the subject of destiny?"

"No," I say. "I don't believe in destiny."

His face, as well-defined as my Cream of Wheat, registers mild surprise. "Not believe in destiny?"

"You make your own destiny," I say. "God helps those who help themselves." I knock over the milk pitcher.

"Have you heard the expression 'Character is destiny?'" my attorney asks.

"No," I say, mopping up. "My character is on trial. That's enough. I don't need a destiny thrown in. It's not part of Walter's complaint. The jury hasn't been asked to consider it. Please. Let's just try to win on the issue of overwork."

For a weak man, my attorney can be surprisingly stubborn. He doesn't argue the point, but when we reach the empty courtroom he pulls a single sheet of paper out of his briefcase.

"Give me some background, please, on *No Certain Home*, Chapter Ten."

"Agnes is at the Berlin depot, leaving on a train for China."

"Why?"

"She has wanted to go to China for years."

"Is she German?"

"American. She's Agnes Smedley, a journalist in the 1920s and 1930s."

"How old is she in this chapter?"

"Thirty-seven."

"How does she earn her living?"

"By writing." The radiators underneath the row of photographs of defunct judges have begun to hiss and clank. I take off my jacket and hang it on the back of the witness seat. Talking about my book makes me warm. The custodian at the tall oak door with his mop and polishing cloths does not appear to be listening. "She was a workaholic. She worked to educate herself, for she did not finish fifth grade. She worked against corruption of the elite. She wrote articles and books about China. She coordinated medical services for the Red Chinese Army. She lectured on—"

"Fine," says my attorney. When I next look up, he is asking the Court to mark Defendant's Exhibit A for identification.

"So marked," says the judge.

My attorney hands me a single sheet of paper. "Will you please read what is written?"

I clear my throat and begin.

Defendant's Exhibit A

"No Certain Home, Chapter Ten.

"Agnes' mind widened, narrowed, widened again, like the space between train cars that lurch against each other, false starts on the trip east. She pressed herself into one corner of her compartment and waited for the train to pull out of the Berlin station.

"Everything she knew about China deserted her. Asia had become a continent not to be talked about, but to be lived. The other half of the world was as near as the other half of herself. It felt like a destiny which she now wished to evade."

"Why did you write a novel about Agnes Smedley?" my attorney asks, approaching the witness box and taking Exhibit A from my hands.

"I read her biography and was fascinated."

"Why was another book needed about this woman?"

"Another book wasn't necessarily needed, but I needed to write the book. Do you understand?"

"No," says my attorney. I feel compelled to explain.

"I wanted to know her, but since she was dead, the next best thing was to try and live with her for as long as it took to write the book."

"How long was that?"

"Three and a half years. I went to China, Germany, and Denmark. Missouri, Colorado, Arizona. I went to San Francisco and San Diego. I followed her wherever I could."

"You took time off from work?"

I beam with pleasure. "Yes. Vacations. Weeks and weeks. I vacationed in China. Also Germany and Denmark. Not to mention Missouri, Colorado—"

"Yes, yes," my attorney says. He does not want to run our strategic point into the ground. I have taken vacations after all. It was just that I didn't consider them vacations.

"If you do not believe in destiny, why did you attribute a destiny to Agnes Smedley?"

"It was a figure of speech," I say. Walter's complaint does not contain the word destiny. This trial is not about the meaning of my life. This trial is about how I conduct it. The judge will surely make a ruling and get us back on track.

My attorney pulls out another sheet of paper with what, in a less plump man, would be a flourish.

"Request Defendant's Exhibit B marked for identification, Your Honor."

"So marked."

Oh, God. Not more writing.

"An excerpt from Chapter Twelve, same book," says my attorney. He has familiarized himself with the story line, because he turns to the jury and says, "It is 1943. Agnes Smedley is back in America after living for many years in China. She lectures widely about her wartime experiences with the Red Army and her belief in the Chinese Revolution. Here we see her addressing students in a small church college in the South."

He hands me the single sheet. I read.

Defendant's Exhibit B

"What made you go to China?" a girl asked after a lecture at a private church school in Mississippi. The auditorium was small. Polished railings, dark oak wainscoting, a mural painted by a regional artist. It was an auditorium of the type to be found in hundreds of small American colleges. Agnes looked up into the balcony at the questioner. The tall, thin girl sounded passionate. Her question carried a charge, as if the answer might have an effect on a choice being made that very day.

"I went to China because" — she paused — "because it was my destiny."

Agnes sat down in the speaker's chair. In the moment of silence before applause began she knew she was one of those who is strong enough to do necessary work. One of those who knows what her work is. About that she had no confusion."

Continued Recross Examination

"Have you ever felt called to be a court reporter?" asks opposing counsel.

"Absolutely not."

"Have you been called to write?"

"No. I choose to write."

"Why?"

"To overcome emptiness."

"What do you mean, *emptiness?* What kind of emptiness?"

"A great nothingness everywhere that we try to disguise with love and religion and activity." It is a murky answer that opposing counsel doesn't wish to explore.

"Explain to the jury the process of writing a novel."

"Well, I spread a part of the world out in front of me, play with it, explore it, people it. I hold it up like a mirror and gaze into it. Then I jiggle it and try to sprinkle the walls with light."

Counsel looks exasperated, but I rather like my fancy answer.

"Have you ever written an irrevocable decision into one of your novels?"

"Oh, yes. Irrevocable. Yes."

My attorney frowns.

"Your Honor," says opposing counsel, "I request Plaintiff's Exhibit One be marked for identification."

"So marked."

Where do these attorneys find my manuscripts?

"Ladies and gentlemen of the jury, I submit Exhibit One as evidence of this witness's belief that individual choice, not destiny, shapes lives."

"Where did you get this?" I ask.

"There is no pending question," says the judge. Motes swirl through the courtroom window on a shaft of afternoon light and settle on His Honor's silver hair and fine-boned face.

I lower my head and focus on the ink-specked paper tape crawling out of my stenotype machine. Paper notes used to be essential. We typed or dictated from them. Now they are mere backup in case the electronics fail. I entertain a thought: could work be like my paper notes? A mere backup to some invisible certainty — call it destiny if you wish — that is quite the opposite of emptiness? Am I working to fill a void that is already filled? Am I not empty after all? Could all the busy-ness, activity, choices, be as superfluous as my paper notes? Just as crowded and spotty as the untranslated ink strokes and characters that will never be read because the real work is being done somewhere else? Am I merely reporting the sound of myself?

Extremely doubtful. Mushily hopeful. Poorly defined terms. I reject the idea as soon as it occurs to me.

"Read Plaintiff's Exhibit One to the jury, please," opposing counsel instructs me. I take the sheet of paper he hands over.

"From *The Absent Woman*." I look at the jury. "The scene is a piano competition in Bellingham, Washington."

Plaintiff's Exhibit 1

The young man now reducing Bach to brilliant rubble, for example, probably had an entire family rooting for him. Possibly a mother who had sacrificed her ego from the day he was born so he could excel; who took every opportunity to make him look good. Possibly he had sisters who deferred to him; watched him glorify his school, his family, himself, on playing fields, in classrooms, in recitals. For without a doubt he was a gifted and confident young man, much used to praise.

True, much would be asked of him. But here was I, and women like me, willing to make choices, take independent action, run obstacle courses, who were yet made to look atypical, confused, wrong, bad, or psychologically unsound, we ambitious women who would seldom have the support that most men take for granted.

No; I was the boy's competitor. Anything that brought me to a peak, that made me deliver my best and more than my best, I would take on. I had chosen to play great music splendidly, and be heard.

"Would you say the woman in this novel has a destiny?" asks opposing counsel.

"She doesn't have a destiny," I answer. "She's making up her life as she goes along. Whatever she's looking for or hoping to gain will not come because it's destined. It will happen because she makes it happen."

Opposing counsel, who looks like a male model in his brown slacks and tweed jacket, puts one hand in his pocket and steps forward for the kill. "If you have no destiny, Madam Reporter, then you have free will. You are free to make a decision in favor of my client. You are free to spend more time relaxing with Walter. Free to be fully alive." He adds a subtle capper. "And you are guilty of not having made that choice already."

My attorney's objection — "Calls for speculation" — is not heard.

"I am working and writing," I cry out, "restless and tense because that is the only way I can accomplish everything that I need to do!"

Opposing counsel steps back and confers with — Walter. Walter has slipped into the courtroom and seated himself at counsel table. As usual, I didn't hear him enter. He is a quiet man. I turn to look at my attorney who is — not here. Who knows how long he's been gone? He left his computer behind. He doesn't like the electronic age.

"Where is esteemed counsel?" asks the judge.

"I have no idea," I say, just as my attorney opens the double oak doors and trots down the aisle with a large book in his hands.

"Present, Your Honor," he says, out of breath. "I was in the library running down some citations."

"I can't imagine any citations applying to this case," mutters the judge. Breaches of decorum and the unorthodox nature of the lawsuit are taking their toll on His Honor.

Opposing counsel pulls once on his tie. He does not look as fresh as we have come to expect. "Your Honor, my client wishes to be heard."

The jury watches Walter rise and approach the witness box. He is actually going to try and speak to me directly. I cannot imagine it will be permitted. But my attorney, who should be objecting, is lost in his book, and the judge has pulled out a silver fingernail clipper that he applies with a subdued *chirp* to the nails of one hand.

"Take your time," he says to Walter.

Walter addresses me formally. "Madam Reporter, could not the idea of a destiny fill the emptiness within?" He takes advantage of my silence. "Since you do not believe you have a destiny, could you not live as *if* you had a destiny, a destiny that is being accomplished every moment, whether you're working or not? Then perhaps you could relax."

I cannot think of a response.

"You have faith in Agnes Smedley's destiny, yet you have no faith in your own."

It is curious. Here in court, in public, I am strongly aware of Walter. Deeply attached. Without touching me, he seems to have his hand on my pulse. I have always loved his hands. My attorney blunders into the precious moment.

"Your Honor" — he opens his book, drops it, bends to pick it up, loses his place, finds it again, and finally begins to read: "'Destiny has more resources than the most imaginative composer of fiction.' By Frank Frankfort Moore."

The judge looks baffled. "Who is Frank Frankfort Moore?" But my attorney is not finished yet. He turns a page and clears his throat.

"'The bullet that will kill me is not yet cast.' Napoleon Bonaparte."

"What is your point?" says the judge.

My attorney looks crestfallen, but only for a moment. "My point is, there is such a thing as destiny, whether my client recognizes it or not." He thumps the book and reaches a new level of fatuousness. "It's right here. Bartlett's *Quotations.*"

"Precisely," says Walter. "Bartlett's *Quotations.* I couldn't agree more with learned counsel." Walter and my attorney have thrown the trial off course — if it was ever on course — by agreeing with each other. "Destiny is a fiction, fiction is belief, and belief is faith."

"Therefore I am," I say sarcastically. I glance at my father and grandfather who never liked sarcasm, especially in women. They are listening to Walter.

"Precisely. Therefore you are. And therefore you can have faith in your writing. You will be published," he says. Walter has never shown this much interest in destiny before. I've never known him to construct a syllogism.

"How long do I have to wait?" We are getting close to the real issues. "It may be someone else's destiny," I whine, "but as for me . . . I'm not getting any younger, Walter."

"Destiny doesn't depend on results," he counters. "Destiny is a fiction. Fiction is belief. Belief is faith. Therefore you are. I, for one, have always known you will be published." He looks pleased with himself, as if he has made a major breakthrough in the lawsuit.

"Destiny requires commitment, Walter."

"You're committed."

"Commitment requires work, Walter."

"No one can accuse you of not working, my dear."

"Furthermore, if I fail, it is utterly final."

"If failure is one's destiny, so be it." Walter is more fatalistic than I. "You fail. Therefore you are."

"I could end up talking to myself, pushing a grocery cart through the streets, believing I am Shakespeare reincarnated and the world is too obtuse to notice."

My attorney steps forward. "That's why we have courts. Every now and then we'll put you on trial, in public, and you can test your perceptions against the prevailing norm. In fact, the courts often set the prevailing norm. Take, for instance, the decision in *Haggerty versus* — "

Oh, no, you don't. I've already sat through too many trials. Heard too many witnesses.

Walter interrupts my attorney. "Your Honor, ladies and gentlemen of the jury, I submit that this witness should stop resisting her destiny, leave the courthouse, and come home and write. If she must report, let her report on herself. If she wants to, she can call it a novel." And he sits down.

Further Redirect Examination

As my attorney steps around the counsel table, he stumbles against his computer and disrupts the realtime function. He doesn't care. Realtime transcription means nothing to him. He has no respect for electronics. Not the slightest interest in the Internet. He has no blog. He ignores social media.

Prompted by Walter, who is whispering in his ear, my attorney asks, "What have you learned from reading your novels?"

Isn't it enough that I've written the darn things? Do I have to read them, too? My attorney is mismanaging my case terribly. Although he is an old friend and I secretly like his dumpy ways, I suspect someday he will be sued for malpractice. A man like him can hardly escape charges.

"I can't be objective about my own writing," I say. "Writing my books has proved nothing to me and I doubt that reading them will, either."

He closes the lid of his useless laptop and asks, "Do you ever feel there is something you are supposed to be doing?"

"Yes. I should be transcribing right now. I'm four jobs behind." I have begun to perspire. Perhaps this trial was destined to be poorly litigated. I certainly didn't choose to have such a kaleidoscope of changing issues. Walter and my attorney have migrated into agreement with each other, while opposing counsel and I seem to hold similar positions, if anyone in this lawsuit can be said to hold a position. I find that I do not want to look at the jury. I am sick to my stomach. I try to leave the witness box, but the judge orders me to stay. He seems to have forgotten I am his court reporter. He's treating me like any other witness. I feel very much like my father now: number one. I really should get some special consideration.

And damn! There goes my attorney again, up the aisle and out the tall oak doors. Walter steps forward to take over redirect. I look up at the judge who pretends not to notice that my legal representation is fluid, to say the least.

"Do you have faith?" Walter asks.

Walter knows I have very little faith.

"You mean, do I believe in something?"

"That's my question."

"Yes, I do."

"What is it?"

The judge and jury are waiting for my answer. I am waiting for my answer.

"I believe in work," I say. It doesn't sound like much of a faith.

"What do you believe in if you have no work?"

"I believe in finding work."

"And if there is no work to be found?"

"Then I will make work. I'll write books that haven't been asked for and won't be read. I'll pick up litter from the streets. Cut old people's toenails. Run errands. Reconcile checkbooks."

Walter smiles. He knows I cannot reconcile checkbooks.

"If you were given the choice between court reporting or writing novels, which would you choose?"

"Writing novels."

"Do you have enough money to live without employment?"

"Not quite."

Walter strolls over to the jury. He looks a lot like Gregory Peck in *To Kill a Mockingbird.* "Do you need as much money as you earn?"

"Well, no. But I'm saving."

"For what?"

"Old age. Unforeseen eventualities."

Walter turns toward the lovely old window and gazes at the sky. He feels isolated. I have left him out of my life. I wouldn't blame him if he walked away with those quiet footsteps. Although it would be days before I looked up from the computer and noticed he was gone, I would miss him terribly.

The Verdict

It is after five. Walter and I are in my office. I should be transcribing, but with the jury down the hall deliberating and the judge waiting for the verdict in chambers, it is difficult to concentrate. I stare out the window, daydreamy, vague, while twelve people sort through the evidence of my life.

I hope my father will not persuade his fellow jurors against me. Yet, at the same time, I hope he has power and influence over everything in his sway, all his life long.

It will be twilight soon. I pick up a magazine. Walter is outside now, leaning on one of the courthouse pillars. I watch him through the window. I can see by the bright glow between his fingers that he's taken up smoking again.

The jury has been deliberating since two o'clock in the afternoon. The evidence must be even more damning than I thought. I imagine the scene. One or two people are holding out in my favor, but they are hungry and tired and the opposition is strong.

No sound of scraping chairs or pounding of a tabletop drifts down the hall.

The New Yorker on my lap is lying open to an article about Vermeer: "Inventing Peace," by Lawrence Weschler. Why couldn't I invent peace instead of a trial? Holland, the author says, was as chaotic in the seventeenth century as Bosnia at the end of the twentieth. Vermeer, he says, tried to construct a quiet place for himself among endless wars and political instabilities by painting canvases filled with calm light and the likenesses of contented, self-sufficient women.

On the facing page just such a woman returns my gaze.

O, Lady of Delft, I have not achieved peace, contentment, or self-sufficiency. Every breath I draw is a judgment on myself. I have sat through too many trials. Heard too many witnesses.

Her voice is well modulated. "Write a book," she says, "about the man who painted me. Very little is known. You will not be limited by facts. I will help you." She is pure expressiveness. I cannot separate my gaze from hers. I have always known her. She is both destiny and choice. She makes me long to write something beautiful, not on a shorthand machine or computer, but in pen and ink. When I finally look up, Walter is standing in the room.

"The building feels empty," he says.

Reluctantly I move from Vermeer's world to my own. I explain that county offices are closed. Staff has gone home. Only he and I, the bailiff, the judge, and the jury remain. I step into the hall. The courthouse does, indeed, feel empty. Since they built the new jail, there are no cells in the basement. I reach for Walter's hand. We step softly toward the jury room.

The door is open. There is no sound of talking. No sound of twelve people discussing me. I look in. The straight-backed chairs are pulled up neatly to the long table. The room is empty. I take a sharp breath and have a coughing fit. Walter pounds me on the back. We walk to the judge's office and knock on the door.

There is no answer. I knock again. Walter turns the knob. It is locked.

"I see what has happened," I say when I have stopped coughing. "There is no verdict, Walter."

"No verdict? We pay all these taxes and there's no verdict?" He rattles the door.

"It is the only trial I know of where the judge and jury left before the proceedings ended," I say. But I am talking to myself. Without a sound, Walter, too, has left the courthouse. He is dispirited. He knows I will always be a driven, obsessed person, whether writing or reporting; that I will never spend as much time with him as he would like. I return to my office, pick up the magazine, and follow him. He's probably already turning on lights, igniting the gas jet in the fireplace, feeding the cat. Soon he will start dinner. Cooking is his way of overcoming sorrow.

The streets between the courthouse and home are familiar. Just now, slightly above the horizon, a star's old light breaks in upon us. I have read there is much burning debris in the universe.

Walter opens the door and I step inside. Just as I thought, he's started the fire. I step nearer.

"Didn't you forget something?" he says. I touch him. He is real. Our cat brushes between us, tail curling around our legs as he pads in a circle around us. "Where's your laptop?"

"At the courthouse," I say. "What have you been doing today?"

"Moi?" He smiles. He likes to pretend he's fluent in French. I trace his lips with my finger. Overwhelmed by a pang of love as intense as infatuation, I momentarily step outside again. Catching my breath, I see my attorney approach in his old Ford. The windows fly down, fly up, fly down. He is still trying to master the remote-control buttons. He asks if I need a ride.

"Thanks, but no," I answer. His driving is legendary, and I want to live. I want to love. He glides on down the street. The bulb above his license plate is burned out, but I can still see the letters as he passes under the streetlight: "YR DESTINY."

At the corner of Fifth and Elm, he stalls. After a few grinding sounds he manages to start the engine again. He will arrive home in time to prepare for court the next day: argument on behalf of an elderly couple cheated of their life savings by a mail order firm out of Miami.

Publication Credits

Inner Passage (first published as 'Passage' in roger, an art & literary magazine, Vol. 2, Spring 2007)

If You Love a Thing (first published in *Rebecca's Road*, Holland House Books, 2013)

Pen-and-Ink (first published in MasticadoresUSA, online journal, January 2023)

The Long Black Cadillac (first published in Armadillo, April 1997, The Maverick Press, Vol. 11)

The Broom (first published in *Uncertain Promise*, Compass Flower Press, 2014)

City of Tomorrow (first published in Southern Humanities Review, Vol. 53.3, Fall 2020)

Acknowledgements

I wish to thank my friends and family for reading many of these stories and commenting on them. Always my sister, Lavetta McCune, first reader. Always, Ella Leffland, friend and writer. Margaret and Jerry Norton, of course. The Cascades Writers' Group, shapers of fiction. Barbara Leonhard: You know why. Alex George, Carrie Koepke, and Skylark. Robert Peett of Holland House Books, editor and publisher of five of my novels. Jocelyn Cullity, a treasured friend and writer who recognizes strength when she sees it. And always, Bill, for his love and beautiful, balanced personality.

— Marlene Lee

Also Available from EIF

Three-Penny Memories, A Poetic Memoir
by Barbara Harris Leonhard

ISBN: 9781739757762

"Do you love your mother?" This provocative question provides the catalyst for this stunning poetic memoir from Pushcart Nominee Barbara Harris Leonhard. Through her artfully crafted poetry, the author considers where her love and loyalties lie following her ageing mother's diagnosis with Alzheimer's.

All Grown Up Now
by Kim M. Russell

ISBN: 9781739404437

This collection of poems opens up a crack in the lining of a poet's life to show what it was like to grow up in a family in the decades after the war, how it shapes the individual, what they learn and keep in their heart, the rituals and routines that are handed down the generations.

In The Shadow of Rainbows
by Selma Martin

ISBN: 9781739404444

In this dazzling debut poetry collection of over 60 carefully selected poems, author Selma Martin points the way to the beauty in the everyday, the shadow of the rainbow, and the silver lining at the edge of every cloud.

My Life With MND
by Daina Mason

ISBN: 9781739404420

In this moving, brave and insightful story, written us-
ing eye-gaze technology, Daina tells of her journey
from first symptoms to diagnosis, and goes on to explain how she has adapted to life with this debilitating
condition. Daina won a BBC Radio Cumbria Make A Dif-
ferece Award for the book.

The Colourblind Grief
by Jude Gorini

ISBN: 9781739404406

A rip-roaring ride of a confessional novel, which takes
place within the gay club scene of East London, before
moving to Europe and the serene, sandy beaches of La
Graciosa. Jude Gorini has written a brave, uncompro-
mising tale which deals with issues of mental health,
sexual identity and self-discovery. Difficult to put
down, and impossible to forget!

Archery in the UK
by Nick Reeves and Ingrid Wilson

ISBN: 9781739757786

Inspired by the *Lyrical Ballads* of Wordsworth and
Coleridge, two authors set out to pen a contemporary
homage to this timeless collection. As the collaboration
progresses, however, the poetry and the unique nar-
rative it carries takes on a life of its own. Thus, the
authors come to tell their story through a collection of
ballads, sonnets, pantoums and other forms.